PINCH

PINCH

by
Larry Callen

Illustrated by Marvin Friedman

An Atlantic Monthly Press Book
Little, Brown and Company
BOSTON   TORONTO

Fourth Printing

T 02/75

Library of Congress Cataloging in Publication Data

Callen, Larry.
    Pinch.

    "An Atlantic Monthly Press book."
    SUMMARY: A boy growing up in a country town becomes
involved with a pig he trains to hunt and a mean,
crafty gentleman who teaches him the art of trickery.
    [1. Pigs—Fiction. 2. Country life—Fiction]
I. Title.
PZ7.C134Pi   [Fic]   75-25618
ISBN 0-316-12495-8

ATLANTIC–LITTLE, BROWN BOOKS
ARE PUBLISHED BY
LITTLE, BROWN AND COMPANY
IN ASSOCIATION WITH
THE ATLANTIC MONTHLY PRESS

*Published simultaneously in Canada
by Little, Brown & Company (Canada) Limited*

PRINTED IN THE UNITED STATES OF AMERICA

To a bunch of Callens

Willa Carmouche Callen
Erin Andree Callen
Alex David Callen
Dashiel Noel Callen
Holly Willa Callen
Emily Barrouquere Callen
Lawrence Willard Callen, Sr.
Mary Dorothy Padgett
David Leo Callen
Ann Victoria Woods
Toni Margaret Sauviac

each for a very special reason

Contents

PINCH

❦ 1 ❦

The Hunting Pig

My name is Pinch Grimball and I live in Four Corners. Maybe you heard of it. Mr. Tony Carmouche's store is there. And there's us Grimballs and Charley Riedlinger and his folks and the Sweet boys. And there's Mr. John Barrow. There's other people, but not too many.

Every now and then something special happens in Four Corners, like the hunting pig contest between my dad and the Sweets and Mr. John Barrow. My dad wins every year. You might not know it, but pigs make good pets if you take time with them. They are smarter than dogs. At least some of them are. My dad says a proper trained pig is better at hunting birds than any hound he ever saw. He's been training them off and on since he was a boy. Way he tells it, the ones he had when he was a boy were so smart they could almost talk. The ones he's had since I been around have been a little on the dumb side, but they still managed to beat out all other Four Corner pigs at bird pointing without really trying too hard. That's 'cause my dad really knows what he's doing. You can't say that for Billy and Henry Sweet. And you sure can't say that for Mr. John Barrow, unless money is involved. Then he's pretty sharp.

Dad says a hunting pig has got to be a little on the skinny side and have some self-control. You don't all the time find that in pigs, so when you are looking for a pig to train you have to look pretty careful.

I found my very first hunting pig when I was walking home from school one blistering hot afternoon. I was so sweaty hot I was thinking hard about jumping feetfirst into a river full of cool water. Blind River is deep and not ten minutes away. It hadn't had a boy in it since yesterday when me and Charley tried swimming underwater to catch a coot by the legs and nearly drowned doing it.

I was in front of Mr. Tony Carmouche's store when I saw this skinny little black and white pig sitting in a smelly wire cage on the front porch. The pig was looking careful at me. I stopped and sat on the steps for a while and watched him and he watched me. Then I went in the store and asked Mr. Tony how much he wanted for the pig.

"Five dollars," he said. "You looking for a new pig for your paw to train, are you Pinch?"

"I'm looking for one for *me* to train," I told him. A boy had never trained a pig in Four Corners before. Maybe I could do it, but I couldn't figure a way in the world for me and that pig ever to take the hunting pig championship away from my dad, 'cause I didn't

have any five dollars and wasn't likely to any time soon.

He sure looked to be the right kind of pig. He was skinny enough. And he had a long snout for sniffing birds. But I didn't have one single penny. That cute little pig kept looking at me and I could tell he was thinking that if it was me in the cage and him out here, he would surely find a way of raising the five dollars. So I thought about it some more.

When I found Dad to tell him about the pig, he was fixing the trigger on a rabbit trap. He said he was getting too old for hunting pigs and he didn't have any plans for risking five dollars on a skinny pig just 'cause it might turn out to be the right kind. Money was short, Mom needed new cooking pots, and he didn't have any time to train a pig anyway, 'cause he was spending his free time fixing his traps. He spent so much time saying no, I thought he would end up saying yes, but he didn't.

"Anyway, Pinch, you already owe me two-fifty in moving picture money which it looks like I'll never get back. You start working that off and then we'll talk about pig money."

"You got to see the little pig, Dad. He's got a real hound look about him."

"You want to start chopping some wood now?"

"I got some place to go. Could we talk about it later?"

"We can talk about it when you decide you want the pig bad enough to do some work to get it." He went back to fixing his traps.

Wanting the pig bad enough wasn't the problem. I wanted the little pig bad enough, but I wasn't too keen about working chores to get it. Not much fun in chopping wood around your own house.

I went out to the road to find something to do but there wasn't a soul anywhere in sight and I didn't find anything to do. Except there was an old tin can in the road and kicking cans is fun, so I kicked it. It clunked into the ditch, so I looked around for another one to kick. When I kicked the next one it rattled like it had a rock in it.

That rock turned out to be a quarter. And that's what started me on the way to making my fortune. It was the first step on the way to that five dollars, that's for sure. Trouble was, it was just a little bitty step. And there were too many tempting twenty-five cent things to do with the quarter, most of them right across the street at Mr. Tony's store. I thought about it for a while. Best thing to do would be to pay the store a visit before I decided whether to save the quarter or spend it.

At Mr. Tony's store you can get gumballs and they're pretty tasty if they don't sit on the shelf for about a year and get hard as a rock. But to show you that things work out for the best most of the time, I never made it to that store. I met Charley Riedlinger on the way.

❦ 2 ❧

Charley Riedlinger

CHARLEY RIEDLINGER's my best friend. He's about a head bigger than me, even though I'm two weeks older than him. He fights pretty good. He hits almost as hard as I do. So we don't have too many fights. About the only thing we *really* disagree on is Jean Laffite. That's the name of this hunk of skull I found last summer near Blind River. I call it Jean Laffite 'cause that's the only pirate name I know. Dad says it looks more like a muskrat skull than a human skull, and that his name couldn't be Jean Laffite anyway 'cause Jean Laffite was a Gulf pirate and this one had to be a swamp pirate, if he really was a pirate. But I don't know. Dad also says swamp pirates didn't fool around riding pirogues like regular Cajuns did. Swamp pirates rode alligators. I don't know as I believe that either.

Charley is always wanting to borrow Jean Laffite, but I won't let him. I told him a hundred times a genuine pirate skull can't be trusted in the hands of a boy. A man has to watch over it. He keeps saying that just 'cause I'm two weeks older than him doesn't make me more of a man. It's hard to make him understand some things.

I never told him, but Jean Laffite isn't really good for much except looking at. I mean, you can't *use* it for anything. But I like having it around as much as you can like having a skull of a dead pirate.

This particular afternoon Charley had gotten out of school before me, 'cause I had to stay a while and talk with the school teacher about the grass snake I brought to school in the morning and loaned to Mary Dorothy Munch. The teacher said putting an old grass snake down the back of a girl's dress wasn't the same as loaning. I don't see it her way, but it's her school.

In the little time I was talking with the teacher, Charley had caught himself a whopper of a frog.

"Pinch, you ever see a frog this size before?" He was holding it up by the hind legs for me to see. It must have been about a foot long. Its eyes were sticking out, taking in everything that was happening. You could see it wasn't too happy about the whole situation. I poked it and it wiggled.

"It's a big one, all right. What you going to do with it?" I was thinking I might like to buy it, 'cause I sell them for pocket money sometimes at the Farmer's Market.

"Why, I'll keep it, or maybe sell it for about a dollar. This is the biggest frog I ever seen, and it's bound to be worth way more than a dollar."

Well, that wasn't so. Even that big a frog wouldn't bring any dollar. I started walking again like I wasn't interested and he followed along.

"Where you going?" he asked.

"Mr. Tony's."

"What for?"

"To get some gumballs."

"How much money you got?"

"I got a quarter."

"Where'd you get it?"

"Found it."

"You didn't find it in front of my house, did you Pinch? 'Cause if you did, it's probably mine."

"Found it near the school."

"Oh. Well, you know I lost a quarter near the school about two years ago. Maybe that's the one it is."

"It's got last year's date on it."

"Oh."

"Charley, you may as well turn around and go on home with your frog, 'cause you won't get any gumballs I buy with this quarter."

"Oh."

"You wouldn't let me have none of that candy your dad brought home from the filling station that time. You remember that, don't you?"

"When was that, Pinch?"

"About six months ago."

He stopped dead and glared at me. "That's not the same at all. I only had about six tiny little bitty pieces of that candy." Then he went into one of his stomping fits and made the dust swirl. But he knew I had him and he didn't push it too far. He didn't turn around and go home either. I started off and he kept following, and every once in a while he would jiggle the frog.

"Pinch, you really got a quarter in your pocket?"

"I do."

"Can I see it?"

Seeing and getting is two different things, so I took it out and showed it to him. He made out like it didn't make any difference it was me who had the quarter instead of him. But then he pulled out the big frog and stuck it under my nose.

"Pinch, I got a good idea. You can have this dollar frog for your quarter. You can have all of him right now. So you just give me the quarter and we'll be settled about this."

The big frog looked at me and I looked at him. I did some fast thinking about gumballs and frogs. It would be a long time before I saw another frog as big as this one, and that gumball jar would be there gathering dust a long time. I stuck out my hand with the quarter, but I might have been too fast doing it 'cause he almost held back giving the frog to me. Finally he did. It wasn't a dollar frog, but it wasn't a quarter frog either. It weighed about two hundred pounds. Maybe neither of us would have traded five minutes later, but it was right to do it then and there. I held tight onto my frog.

"All right now Charley, let's go and get them gumballs," I told him and started out toward Mr. Tony's store.

"Pinch, you are welcome to come with me and *get* the gumballs, but I plan to chew them all by myself."

Now you can't get any meaner than that! He was going to use my own money to buy gumballs with and not let me have any. If that was the way it was going to be, I wasn't even going to walk with him to the store. I told him I hoped the gumballs were solid rock and I was thinking hard of switching best friends to Mary Dorothy Munch. And then I left him right where he was. I stomped off the road and cut across the pasture to Mr. John Barrow's house.

✤ 3 ✤

Mr. John Barrow

MR. JOHN BARROW is better company than Charley anyway, and he's partial to frogs so I knew he'd want to see this whopper.

Some days things just keep happening, one after the other, and this was one of them. Mr. John Barrow was standing beside his chopping stump with a fat chicken in one hand and a hatchet in the other. The chicken's days were numbered.

I guess I better tell you about Mr. John Barrow, 'cause he's hard to believe. He's tall and skinny, with spidery legs. His clothes are all leftovers from his paw, who weighed about a hundred pounds more than him. Those clothes hang on him like bat wings. And the rest of his looks won't get him far either. He's got dark splotches under his eyes like he's been awake all night hanging from the barn rafters.

Mr. John Barrow is a crafty one. Him and me tangled more than once, and it's hard staying ahead of him. He sold Dad some blackberry wine last summer that turned out to be sour as vinegar. He swore he sold it in good faith and put all the money in the church

poor box, and "We wouldn't want to have to ask the preacher to give it back, would we?"

You can trace Mr. John Barrow's craftiness back to his paw who has passed on now. His paw was a mean one who probably never smiled a single time in his whole life. That's what my dad says. But even with all his meanness and craftiness, me and Charley spend a lot of time at his house, mainly 'cause Mr. John Barrow doesn't fool around telling us to "do this" and "don't do that" like most grown ups do.

I held the big frog behind me so I could surprise him with it. With all the worry he had on his face, he could use a surprise or two.

"Pinch, I'm glad to have your company. It's been so bad around here this morning, I'm talking to the chickens again. And there ain't much fun in that." He began telling me about the leak in the roof and that one of his mules was sick and that there were worms in his tomatoes. He stuck the clucking chicken under his arm and walked over and sat on the edge of his porch. I went with him, keeping some distance between us so he wouldn't see the frog. He had a live porcupine in a box on one end of the porch and I didn't get too close to it either.

Mr. John Barrow's biggest problem turned out to be the chickens.

"Son, I'm fixing dinner, but I tell you, I ain't got the stomach or the heart to kill this here chicken. I had chicken for supper every night this week, and I'm wait-

ing for the feathers to sprout. Worst part of it is, each
of them chickens has looked up at me at the very last
minute before they went, like they was asking me how
I had the heart to do them in. I don't care much for
chicken killing. It don't do a thing for my appetite."

"Why don't you eat something else?"

"Well, Pinch, you know I ain't a rich man. I got
to dine on what is available. And since I got all them
chickens back there, why it's more likely than not I'll
be eating more eggs and chickens than I'd really care to."

"Mr. John Barrow, if you had your choice of food
for supper, what would you want on your table?"

"I guess a beefsteak and some potatoes would taste
about as good as anything." He closed his eyes, thinking about the beefsteak sizzling in the pan. "I'm sure
of it, Pinch. That's what I'd really like."

Right then the frog twitched and let out a "Croak!"
I wasn't expecting it to try and get into the conversa-
tion. Mr. John Barrow's eyes popped open. He looked
at me bug-eyed, and then he hunched his skinny shoulders and turned snake-eyed and you could tell he was
thinking hard. I had both my hands behind my back
to make sure the frog didn't give a jump.

"What you got in your hands, Pinch?" he hissed,
snake-eyed.

"Oh, nothing." Wouldn't be much of a surprise if
I let him get it out of me just by asking.

"You know, Pinch. I been doing some more thinking about that beefsteak. I don't know if that's what

I really want anyway. You know what I really think I want for supper?"

"What?"

"Course, I wouldn't pay a lot of money to git one."

"Get what?"

"They ain't worth much money, you know, Pinch."

"What color are they?"

"Maybe a dime, that's about all."

"Mr. John Barrow, you better tell me what you arc talking about so both of us will know."

"Pinch, is that a skinny old ten-cent frog you got hiding behind you?"

"No ten-cent frog behind me," I told him. It was worth a lot more than any ten cents. I had come here only to show Mr. John Barrow the big frog. But if he was tired of chicken as he said he was, I might make a sale right here. If he wanted to eat frog legs for supper, that was all right with me.

"Pinch, if it *was* only a ten-cent skinny frog, what would you want for it. No market for frogs now days, son. You know that."

I was starting to look fondly on the chicken under his arm. One frog for one chicken would be about right, with the fellow who got the chicken coming out just a mite on top. But knowing Mr. John Barrow, he wouldn't see it that way. So I played the game the way he always played it.

"Well, if I *did* have a frog, maybe I'd take about ten chickens for it." I waited for him to jump about a mile at that, but he didn't even blink. He just stared down his skinny nose at me.

"Son, now that's poor bargaining. You got to come down on your terms. What would you really take? Bargaining's like fishing, Pinch. You got to have sprightly bait on your line if you expect to get a nibble."

"Five chickens!" But that didn't shake him either. He didn't even hold tighter onto the chicken.

"Now that's better. You learning." I surely never expected to hear him talk like that. The problem about bargaining with Mr. John Barrow is that he changes his ways on you. When you get his method figured out, he shifts it. That's why he comes out ahead more often than not. But I'd found out he wanted the frog before we started bargaining. So I knew I could lick him this time if I played it careful.

"Pinch, I tell you what I'm going to do. What would you say to three chickens for a skinny frog that maybe you got behind you?"

My fortune was made! I could sell three chickens for fifty cents apiece practically anywhere. Owning the little pig was getting closer by the minute. I never knew getting rich would be so easy. Then I looked Mr. John Barrow square in his twitchy snake eyes and began having my doubts about it being easy. He had a pleasant look on his face like he was being honest about it all. But that didn't mean too much. Either he was getting crafty on me or eating all that chicken had made him lose his bargaining powers. I decided to get while the getting was good.

"Mr. John Barrow, take a look a this," and I flipped the big frog around front for him to see. "Now, where's my three chickens?"

He straightened up to take a look at the frog and a big smile spread on his face. "That's a mighty big frog, Pinch. You know, now that the bargaining is settled, I don't mind telling you I don't think I ever saw one so big before." He reached out to take hold of the frog, but I figured I'd hold onto it until he came up with the chickens. He led me over to the chicken yard and let loose the lucky chicken that didn't make it to his dinner table. Then he went into the hen house and when he came out, he was smiling bigger than ever.

"Look at this Pinch. Look what I got here for you!"

What he had was two furry yellow little chicks, each one about as big as a yellow lemon.

"I couldn't find any more than this, Pinch. But I knew you'd settle for two when you saw these cute little critters."

But he was wrong about that!

"Mr. John Barrow, those are baby chicks, not chickens! They aren't worth but about a nickel apiece!"

"Son, these two will grow up to be something a lot bigger than that silly frog you traded me for them." He stuck one skinny hand out with the two little chicks shivering in his palm and the other skinny hand started grabbing for my frog, but I wasn't about to trade with him when he changed the bargain all of a sudden.

"Pinch, you can't back out on me now. I'm really looking forward to frog legs for supper. I really am,

Pinch. You take these two chicks and do right by them. I know you'll do that, Pinch, 'cause you're a good boy. I always said that." He grabbed out for the frog again, but I was getting mad now and I stepped back from him.

"The price has gone back to five chickens, Mr. John Barrow. And I mean big ones."

"Son, that's too high. You got to come down. If you want, we'll bargain some more. I tell you what. I'll give you one big chicken, a really big one. The biggest one I can find."

"Five!"

"One almost as big as a turkey, Pinch?"

"Five!"

"I'll make it two, Pinch. Two skinny ones."

"Two fat ones!"

"I'll make it medium-sized, Pinch. But I can't do any better than that."

"Done!" I said and stuck out the frog and headed for the chicken yard to pick out my own two chickens.

Now that's what I call good trading. When Mr. John Barrow is down to sucking on frog bones, he might start regretting letting me get the best of him this time. But by then it would be too late, 'cause I wouldn't have his chickens anymore. I was edging my way toward a pig.

❧ 4 ❧

Mr. Tony Carmouche

It was pretty certain I could get fifty cents apiece for the two chickens at the Farmer's Market. That would give me a dollar toward the little pig. Then I'd find four more dollars some place and buy the pig and get Dad to teach me to train it to be a hunting pig.

I walked up to Mr. Tony's store with those chickens under my arms. The pig was still sitting in his cage and not too happy about it. Mr. Tony was at the counter, opening a cardboard box and stacking cans of beans on a shelf. He's the only storekeeper in Four Corners, so I knew we might be eating those beans someday. He's also the only postmaster and the only deputy sheriff. Reason he's got all those jobs is he's a city man with more schooling than he really needs. That's the way with city people. He stopped working when I came in and it looked like he was glad to have a reason to quit. He's a little man and working doesn't come natural to him. That's what my dad says.

"Those are mighty fine hens you got there, son. They belong to your paw?" He was nodding his gray head up and down, answering his own question.

"No. They are all mine."

"You want to sell them?"

"Maybe."

"I'll give you thirty-five cents apiece for them."

"I can get fifty at the Farmer's Market."

"Well, good luck to you." He went back to unpacking the beans.

"Mr. Tony, I want to talk business with you."

"All right." But he kept on working.

"You remember last summer when you let me work in the store? For money?"

"You did a good job, Pinch. But I don't know if I need any help right now." But he stopped his work and was thinking about it. "One thing, though. I'm going to paint one of the back rooms. You could help do that."

"You mean I could do the painting?" That sounded like the kind of work I'd be good at. Don't get a chance to do painting every day. My dad won't let me paint at home since the time I accidentally spilled a bucket of white paint over his black Sunday shoes. It was a Saturday at the time. He said it wouldn't have been so bad if it had been either black paint or a Monday. Mr. Tony didn't seem too keen on me doing any of the real painting either.

"What I'll need help on is moving things around and maybe stirring the paint and cleaning the brushes and things like that. But maybe you can do some of the painting, too. We'll see. Are you interested, Pinch?"

It didn't sound too exciting, but I did want the money to buy the pig.

"What would the job pay?"

"Well, what about fifteen cents an hour? That's what you got last summer."

"But that was a long time ago. I'm almost a year older than I was then."

"Well, what about twenty cents an hour. Is that about the right pay for someone as old as you are now?"

"Could you make it twenty-five?"

"I don't think I could."

"Well . . . O.K. When do we start?"

"I'll let you know. It will be in a couple of days."

"I sure could use some money right now."

"Well, son, why don't you sell me those chickens. Since you are now an official employee of the store, I'll even raise the price to forty cents. Save you the trouble of going all the way to the Farmer's Market."

"But I'll lose twenty cents that way."

"Well, I'd say it's about a twenty cent walk from here to there."

"Could you make it an even ninety cents for the two of them?"

"I could do that," he said. He took the chickens and put them in a box and then he gave me my ninety cents. It jingled good in my pocket.

"I'll let you know in a day or so about the painting work, Pinch." Then as I was almost out of the door he yelled for me to come back, and that's when it happened. "Son, I been meaning to ask you and I almost forgot. You interested in buying that little pig on the porch?"

"I don't have any five dollars." But I was working on it.

"Well, I guess it's about time I changed the price. It's down to two-fifty now. That pig's been around the store long enough. The place is beginning to smell."

"Mr. Tony, I would really like to have it. But I got ninety cents in my pocket. That's every penny I have anywhere in the whole world."

"Well, Pinch, I wouldn't do this for just anybody, but you and me are friends, and you work for the store every now and then and your maw does all her business here except once a month when she goes into town to trade with them sharpies. All that considered, you just give me that ninety cents back and you can have that pig."

This was my day! It started with empty pockets and kicking cans and now I was the owner of a five dollar pig. It all happened so fast it was hard to believe. I gave him his money back and picked up the cute little pig and gave it a hug and a kiss. Him and me were going to be hunting pig champions of Four Corners.

"Pinch, as one businessman to another, I'm going to give you some good advice. Now that you got your pig, you ought to forget all about keeping him skinny and training him as a hunter. You ought to think about fattening him up and selling him at the Farmer's Market. There's good money in that."

"Mr. Tony, how much you figure this little pig would be worth if I fattened it up and sold it at the Farmer's Market?"

"Maybe fifty dollars if you did a good job of it."

I headed out the door again.

"I'll let you know about the painting, Pinch," he yelled.

That made me stop and do some thinking. Working's all right, but I'm not partial to it.

"Mr. Tony, I got to tell you something. The reason I wanted work was to get this little pig. Now that I got it, maybe I don't need to do any work. I'm either going to keep it skinny so it can become a champion hunting pig or I'm going to fatten it up and sell it and then I'll have all the money I'll ever need."

"You'll need money to buy feed, son. You can make up your mind when I'm ready to start painting."

"O.K., but I'm going to be busy most of the time with this pig." And I headed for home to start doing it. But I didn't get there.

❦ 5 ❦

The Sweet Boys

I WAS WALKING down the road as fancy as was possible with a pig under my arm, thinking about what I would do with the fifty or maybe a hundred dollars I'd get for the pig when it had grown up. I didn't see the Sweet boys coming until I was up on them. Billy Sweet was leading a mule tied with an old piece of rope and Henry Sweet was walking alongside the mule, giving it a hit with a willow switch every now and then. Henry had a bucket of blackberries in his hand and he was eating them while he walked. The mule was taking its time. It wasn't a happy mule, you could see that right away. It would be kind of hard to be a happy mule if you belonged to the Sweet boys.

Billy and Henry were big, husky creatures and nice as could be most of the time. They were always laughing and giggling and having fun like little kids, even though they were grown men and Henry even had himself a wife. If those two were to get ahold of any whiskey, that made them even sillier. When they were whiskeyed up, if there wasn't any fun just laying around for the taking, they weren't above stirring some up. They would play tricks on you one day

and then the next day when they sobered up, they
would come around and say they were sorry and
wouldn't do it again.

You should have been there the time they were
pretty drunk and Billy Sweet went into Mr. Tony's
store and started talking about how he could feel in
his bones that snow was coming. Now, it doesn't snow
around here but about once every ten years, so Mr.
Tony knew Billy was pulling his leg. But while they
were talking, that old Henry Sweet snuck into the
store and stole a hundred pound sack of flour and
snuck out again. He climbed on the roof of the store
and started sprinkling flour down past the window.
When Billy saw it coming, he yelled to Mr. Tony,

"Look a here! I told you so!"

But Mr. Tony wasn't anybody's fool and he knew
the difference between snow and flour, so he ran outside to see what was going on. When he saw Henry
Sweet squatting up there on the roof with a silly grin
on his face and a part-empty hundred pound sack of
flour at his side, Mr. Tony just had to laugh too. But
then he saw it was *his* sack of flour that was doing
the snowing and he turned around and hit Billy right
on the jaw. When Henry came down he hit him on the
jaw, too. Knocked both of them flat. Don't guess he
could have done it if they weren't drunk, but they
were.

I saw all of it, 'cause I was standing right there with
Mr. John Barrow when it happened. Mr. John Barrow

wasn't too keen on this kind of joking, although he liked his fun now and then. He kept quiet about it until Mr. Tony laid them out, and then he told him, "You shouldn't a done that, 'cause they are drunk." And Mr. Tony said, "That's fine for you to say, 'cause it wasn't your flour."

But today, walking down the road with the mule, the Sweets didn't look drunk. Fact is they looked almost pleasant. I nodded as we started to pass, but Billy seemed keen on talking.

"Hello, Pinch," he said. "That's a mighty fine looking pig you got there. What's his name?"

"Don't have a name. I just got him." I was more interested in getting home than standing there talking, but they stopped and so did the mule. So I didn't have any choice but act polite and stop, too.

"How you like this mule, Pinch? Ain't it a fine specimen of mulehood?"

It was the sorriest looking mule I had ever seen. It was swaybacked and full of barbed-wire scars. It didn't have a tooth in its mouth and it didn't look bothered about it at all. The scrawny tail looked like someone had pulled all the hair out to make a banjo or something. There were more than a regular share of flies buzzing around, but the tail wasn't doing much of a job chasing them away. A fly would land and the tail would go "Whack!" and the fly would just sit there not paying it any mind. If I was ever a mule I wouldn't want to be this one.

"It's a pretty sorry looking mule," I told them. "Looks just like one of Mr. John Barrow's sorry old mules. Where did you get it?" Henry and Billy Sweet never had a mule before. I wouldn't be at all surprised if they stole it from somewhere. But if they did, they wouldn't tell me. They'd make up some long story to cover up.

"Well, Pinch, that's a long story," said Billy. "You ain't going to believe this, but a stranger was walking along the road and he was looking for some honest person to give a mule to. I told him he had found the right person, and I pointed at Henry. " 'Henry is as honest as they come,' I told him. But Henry wouldn't have none of that. Henry pointed to me and told the stranger I was even honester than he was. So the stranger said if we was all that honest, we must be the ones he ought to give the mule to. So he did." Billy was smiling real big now, like he was proud of himself for being so honest, or for thinking up his story so quick, whichever.

"We ain't got no use for a mule, 'cause we don't even have a plow for it to pull. We're going to sell it cheap to someone who really needs it. Your paw need a good mule, Pinch?"

If he did, I didn't see a good mule around here. "My dad doesn't need a mule," I told him.

"We ain't asking much. Why, this here is a hundred dollar mule, but we would let it go at a bargain."

"It might have been a hundred dollar mule one time, but it has aged some since then," I told them.

"You think your paw would want to pay twenty-five dollars for this mule, Pinch?"

"Billy Sweet, my dad's got his right mind. He doesn't need a mule and he wouldn't buy a sorry looking mule like that for twenty-five dollars if he did need one."

Those Sweet boys just never give up. "Do you need a mule, Pinch?"

"What would I do with a mule?"

"You could sell it," Henry said. He was still eating those blackberries and his mouth was all purply. He was being pretty messy about it. But he started me thinking about my fortune again. Maybe the easiest way to get rich wasn't fattening up the pig after all. Maybe it was mule selling that would do it for me. They were asking twenty-five dollars for the mule, but they'd probably take a lot less. And I had this five dollar pig I paid ninety cents for.

"How much money you got, Pinch?" Billy asked.

"I don't need a mule," I told him. No use getting interested too fast.

"Son, I don't think you see the possibilities in this bargain. Why, you would be the only boy in Four Corners who had his own mule. You just think of the farmers who would come flocking to you to get a chance to buy this handsome mule." That poor mule was just standing there, swishing his tail and missing flies. It was easy to see he wasn't worried about farmers flocking to get the chance to hitch him to a plow.

"I don't have any money at all."

"Oh . . ."

"All I got is this twenty-five dollar pig here under my arm," I told him. I gave the little pig a poke and he perked up and started wiggling like a twenty-five dollar pig. I didn't want him thinking of himself as a ninety cent pig, 'cause it would show on his face. It's likely that Billy and Henry were ahead of me thinking about trading the mule for the pig, 'cause it didn't surprise them any when I brought it up. Fact is, they were acting like they weren't interested at all, which was a sure sign that they were.

"You can't trade a twenty-five dollar pig for a hundred dollar mule, Pinch. Now, you ought to have learned that in school," said purply Henry.

Then Billy nudged Henry aside and said, "But if you want this fine mule bad as that, we are going to let you have him and just take a big loss. You take hold of the mule and get him into the shade quick, 'cause he might get sunstroke standing here in the sun."

But now that I had a chance to go into the mule business, I wasn't too sure of the right thing to do. Did I want to get rich selling mules or did I want to stick with hunting pigs? Wasn't any doubt I could do whichever I wanted. If a fellow can go from nothing to a mule in the course of one afternoon, he surely is destined to make his complete fortune in not too long a time. I might even want to go in partners with my dad, or even Charley. Then all of us could be rich.

Just then the mule decided he wanted a rest and he

sat down on the ground. Then he laid out to take a real
good rest. Henry Sweet tugged on the rope, but the
mule wasn't having any of it. He wasn't only the sorriest
mule I had ever seen. He was the orneriest.

About that time, along came Mr. John Barrow looking
pretty content and picking his teeth with a piece of stick.

"That was a mighty good tasting frog, Pinch. I wish
you could of had some. But there wasn't even enough
for me." Then he saw what was on the end of the rope
Henry was holding on to. "The mule is looking poorly,
Henry." He bent over the mule and prodded it here and
there, but the mule was still set on resting and wouldn't
move.

I told him I needed some advice about changing into
the mule business, as I was planning to trade in my pig
for the Sweets' mule. Henry and Billy kept waving their
arms around like they didn't want me to say anything to
Mr. John Barrow about it, but since we had already
come to terms, I didn't see any harm in it.

Mr. John Barrow heard me out and then wrinkled
his brow like something was worrying him. He looked
at them and he looked at me. "Pinch, I'm sorry to be the
one to tell you, but that's my mule that's laying there."

There he goes again! First he ate my frog and now
he wants my mule! I jumped between him and the mule
so he could see he had a fight on his hands if he tried
to get it.

"Don't git excited now, Pinch. You can have him
if you really want him. Fact is, he really ain't mine no

more. I gave Henry and Billy a bucket of blackberries to take him out and shoot him. He was a pretty sorry piece of mule. But no need to do that now, 'cause he's gone to mule heaven by hisself. He's passed on, son. You don't really want to trade now, Pinch. You'd be trading your pig for a dead mule."

Well, I wasn't ready to hear that. We all took a good look at the mule and gave him a few pokes, and he had passed on, sure enough. The Sweet boys weren't any too happy about Mr. John Barrow letting me in on it though. They got pretty upset about it. First they wanted me to keep the bargain, but there wasn't a chance of me swapping a live pig for a dead mule. Then they wanted Mr. John Barrow to buy back his dead mule, since they couldn't trade with me. But he wouldn't do it. Fact is he had an idea it should be the other way around. Since the mule went up and died on its own, the least they could do was give him back his bucket of blackberries. The three of them kept it up until I got tired of hearing all the yelling, so I just left them there.

That dead mule was the start of something. Deputy Sheriff Tony listened to both stories and then made the Sweets bury the mule, and that got them madder still. From then on the Sweet boys were riled up about Mr. John Barrow and him about them, though it never seemed to me that either of them had any cause to be riled. It was me who almost traded a live pig for a dead mule.

❦ 6 ❧

Mr. Will Grimball

Wʜᴇɴ ɪ ɢᴏᴛ ʜᴏᴍᴇ I went looking for Dad to show him the little pig. He was on the back porch, fitting a new handle to the broken hoe, but when he saw me and the pig he put the hoe down. For a long time he just stared at the pig. Then he broke off staring and looked at me.

"You were right, Pinch. He has the nose of a hunting pig. And he's got a smart look about him." The pig just kept still in my arms, taking it all in. But I wasn't interested in hearing any more about it 'cause this little pig was going to be the start of me making a fortune. Once he started getting fat, his nose would get fat too, and that would finish him as a hunting pig.

"He'd never make it as a hunting pig, Dad. Why he won't even stop his wiggling around for one single minute. He's just a plain old fidgety pig." But the little pig wasn't helping me out a bit. He was as calm as he could be, looking right at my dad like he knew that being a hunting pig was a lot better than being a cooking pig.

I told Dad that I had traded hard to get the little pig.

And I told him that a pig wasn't a fit pet for a boy. I just wanted to keep him long enough to fatten him up, and then I'd sell him for a lot of money and pay off everyone I owed, including him. Dad just stood there listening.

"Mmmm," he said and kept staring. He walked around me and took a look at the pig from another direction. His hands were on his hips like when he's looking at a tree to decide how he ought to cut it to make it fall where he wants.

"Mmmm," he said.

That was all he said. When Mom called us to supper, I penned the pig and washed my hands before she had to tell me. I told her about how I had got the little pig to fatten up so that I could make my fortune. She said that was nice. Dad didn't say another word. He just ate. But I knew what was on his mind. What he was doing was thinking about hunting pigs.

After supper I asked if I could be excused to go and tell Charley about the pig.

"Pinch, let's go sit out on the porch for a minute, I want to talk to you," Dad said. "If you want to go and get the little pig, you can do it." So I did. And then the three of us sat, looking at one another.

"Pinch, you know I sold last year's pig at the Farmer's Market so we could get the lumber to fix this very porch we are sitting on." I said I knew it. "And Pinch, you know I told you about how I had a pig a lot like this one when I was a boy. I had more fun with that pig.

We chased birds all day long." Then he stopped looking at the pig and looked across the road, thinking about chasing all those birds. I guess he was also thinking about how he won the hunting pig contest every year for I don't know how long. Every year the prize is a big ring, specially made by Mr. Tony. Dad has a drawer full of them. Each ring is about as big around as my fist and Mr. Tony says it's a genuine copy of the kind of ring Four Corners people used to put in a pig's nose to have something to tie onto when they were leading the pig to market.

"It's made out of genuine gold," Mr. Tony tells all the kids, but we know different. My dad says the rings are made out of genuine copper, which is a lot easier to come by than genuine gold.

"It's not gold or copper that makes the difference, Pinch. First, its winning the hunting pig contest. When you win you know you got a better pig and you did a better job at training than anybody else. And next, Tony puts a lot of work into making those rings. You go watch him once and you'll see how hard that kind of work is. That's what makes the ring something worth winning."

Dad kept at his thinking for a while longer. Then he turned to me and said, "Pinch, let's keep the pig and I'll train him. We'll both get a lot of fun out of it."

"But I want to use the pig to make some money."

"Well, I'll tell you what. How about selling him to me? How much you figure he is worth?"

"Mr. Tony was asking five dollars for him."

"How much did you give for him?"

"I gave two chickens worth about five dollars."

"They must've been some chickens. And what did you give for the chickens?"

"A five dollar frog."

"Son, you been trading even right along. You got to learn something more about business. Seems like more of John Barrow ought to have rubbed off on you by now." He had started looking at the little pig again. "Now, tell me, what did you give for the frog?"

"Some money."

"How much?"

"A quarter."

"You did pretty good on the frog trade, Pinch."

I didn't tell him I had even found the quarter.

"I tell you what, Son. I'll make you a fair offer for the pig. I'll offer you two-fifty for him. That's ten times more than the quarter you started out with. What do you say about that?"

Two-fifty would be more real money than I had actually seen during all of the trading. And I was just about to tell Dad that he had himself a deal when he said, "You give me the pig and we'll be square on the moving picture money."

"What!" I jumped up and held tight onto the little pig.

"You heard me, Pinch. Hand over the little pig. Boys got to pay their debts, same as everybody else."

"But I've been trading hard all day long to get this little pig. I'm planning on fattening him up and selling him and getting rich and having chocolate bars whenever I want to. You going to spoil all that just 'cause of a few silly moving pictures? I didn't even like them when I saw them." He hadn't said a single word about pigs when he loaned me the money in the first place. "Dad, you know what I had to do to get this little pig? I had to kick the right can to get the quarter. That was the start. And I had to outdo Mr. John Barrow at his bargaining game to get the chickens. And if the Sweets had their way, I would be sole owner of a gravestone with a dead mule under it." I was hugging tight onto the pig, but Dad's big hands were reaching out to get him. I tell you, my throat was tight and my eyes were watery and I was swallowing hard to keep back the tears. This was the unhappiest day in my whole life. You won't catch me in the moving pictures again, even if it's free.

"Cut out the foolishness now, Pinch, and let me have the pig." Then he pulled it from me and cradled it in his arms. The little pig didn't know what was happening and he looked kind of scared. Dad gave him a smile like he was saying, "I saved you from the cooking pot." Then he gave me a hard look and told me again how a person has to learn to pay off his debts, one way or the other.

"This'll teach you a good lesson, Pinch." And he kept on going like that, telling me how his getting my pig was going to be good for me. He told me that getting two-fifty for the pig meant I was making a big profit on it after all, and maybe I really was meant to find my fortune soon. But I wasn't interested in hearing all that. Wasn't any money jingling in my pockets. Talk's not money.

"And, I tell you what, Pinch. Just so that you have something to start you on your way again, I'm going to throw in a real cash quarter. That makes it two-seventy-five you are getting for your pig."

Now he was trying to make it sound like the twenty-five cents was going to make me a rich man and the chocolate bars were just around the corner. I started arguing some more, but he was getting tired of it.

"That's it, Pinch. This trading is finished. I'm going to keep this pig and make you a debt-free boy. Now get along and tell Charley whatever you were going to tell him."

🌿 7 🌿

Homer

MY DAD named the little pig Homer, which is the name of a fat uncle of his. Dad started Homer in training the very same day he took him off of me. I wouldn't have a single thing to do with that pig from the very beginning. He wanted the pig, he could keep him. I wouldn't water him and I wouldn't feed him. I wouldn't even wave hello at him. About the third day of training Dad and the pig came in from the field and over to the porch where I was sitting. I pretended I didn't even know Homer was there.

"Pinch, it probably would be a good idea for you to start learning something about pig training. Why don't you come out with us. I want Homer to spend more time getting used to the smell and feel of the grass and the woods."

He hadn't ever asked me to help him train a pig before, and to tell the truth, I liked the idea but I didn't let on right away.

"Maybe so," I said and stood up slowly. Pig training is usually for grown-ups and even some of them don't do it too good. If I wasn't due to make my fortune just yet by selling pigs, at least I would be the only boy in Four Corners who knew something about pig training. So I went.

The little runt pig really took to the field. He held close to us for the first few minutes. From then on it was us that had to keep up with him. It was kind of funny, 'cause some of the birds the little pig was supposed to be stalking were bigger than him. And the first time Homer jumped a rabbit, it was hard to tell who was hunting who. The rabbit sat there and thought about it for a while before he decided to run.

"Pinch, there's a couple of things you got to know about pig training right at the start. You know a little about dog training. Well, pig training ain't much different. But you got to remember that a dog *wants* to please you and is only looking for a way to do it. Ain't that way with a pig. Most pigs don't care one way or the other. They are stubborn. You find a pig that takes to you as a man, you got yourself a special pig. So, your first job in pig training is to get the pig to like you. That's rule number one. And rule number two is when you are in the field working your pig, you got to make it fun for him. Pigs don't like chores any more than boys do."

We didn't stay out long that first morning. Dad said it was best to keep the lessons short but regular until the pig started enjoying them. Next morning Dad put a little leather harness on Homer with a bell on it so as we could keep better track of him if he went

off and rolled in the bushes like he did sometimes. Day
after that he tied a rope on the harness, and before
the week was out Dad had him walking at his side and
Homer would go or whoa whenever Dad said to. Dad
would make the rope longer every day or so and in
a couple of weeks that pig was dragging about 100
feet of light line behind him. Dad would call him in.
If he didn't come, Dad would give a jerk on the line,
and after a while Homer got the message and would
come back almost every time. Then Dad took off the
rope and the harness and we had us a partly trained,
stubborn pig.

All the time Dad and me were training him Homer
kept getting bigger. He even started losing some of his
stubbornness. Every time Homer did what he was
supposed to Dad would tell him what a great pig he
was. Mom didn't think he was so great, and she didn't
make any secret about it. One of her reasons was a
pretty good one. She had put a freshly baked apple
pie on the window sill to cool and Homer had climbed
on a box and got at it. Mom came storming out the
back door with a broomstick in her hand, but Dad
told her that nobody had actually *seen* Homer eat
the pie. It could have been a coon or a possum. Mom
said that coons and possums were night creatures and
her pie got eaten in the middle of the day and that
pig better stay away from the house if it knew what
was good for itself.

Dad is always one to make the best out of something bad and as soon as Mom went inside he turned to me and said, "Now, Pinch, what did you learn out of all that?" I didn't see anything that was worth learning except maybe that he should have blamed the pie eating on a dog or a cat instead of a coon or a possum. So I told him that.

"Son, you got to keep your eyes open. We've been having trouble with that pig ourselves. Ain't that right?"

I told him it was.

"But now we got him where we want him."

Well, I didn't understand that.

"Son, what do we know about Homer now that we didn't know before?"

"Well, we know he likes apple pie." I was spoofing, but he picked me right up on it.

"That's exactly right. So we got him right where we want him. From now on when we go out in the field we bring along some apples. And every time he does what we want him to do, we give him a hunk of apple. We got us a winner now, Pinch."

And that's what we did. Next day Dad started teaching Homer to fetch a stick when he threw it and every time Homer would bring it back he got a hunk of apple. That pig really liked apples. Only time he balked was when Dad threw the stick into some sticker bushes. So Dad walked right into those bushes himself and when Homer saw there wasn't anything to it more than a thorn or two and some cockleburs, he followed right behind.

That's about the time the pig training fever started getting to me. I was tired of watching and told Dad I wanted to help. So the way we worked it was that Dad would start things out to make sure both Homer and me understood what had to be done. Then he would leave us out in the field and go home to do his work. Homer and me would practice. And sometimes Charley would come out and he would do the watching.

There's only one bad thing about training a pig in a cow pasture, and that's cows. There is nothing more curious than a cow. A dozen of them would be way over on the other side of the field just laying down in the shade and chewing away. Then they would see us working and one by one they would come ambling over to get in the way and find out what was going on. While they stood there just looking, Homer would stand there looking back. Then the cows would get tired watching us watching them and would move off. About ten minutes after we started working again, they would come walking back to see why we were still fooling around in their pasture. There isn't a cow living that ever took a prize for being smart.

The day we took Homer out for his first real hunt, the cows kept their distance 'cause Dad brought a dog along. If Homer was going to learn how to really find birds, he ought to learn from someone who knew first hand. Dad borrowed Mr. Tony's pointer. That pointer knew what he was doing, even if he wasn't the best in the business. Now, Homer had gotten used to following scents, and the dog was no stranger to him, so there weren't any problems at first. But the first time the dog actually pointed a bird, Homer just sat there and watched, his head cocked over to one side.

"You see there, Pinch? He's sitting when he should be working. Never let your pig sit when he's in the field. There's enough time for him to sit around home in his pen."

That's when we got ourselves a helper. Dad told me to tell Charley to get over to our house first thing in the morning. When it was time to go the three of us followed the pig and the hound out into the field. Dad was holding a willow switch in his hand.

"Now, boys, here's what we're gonna do. We're gonna team up on the pig. Pinch and I will hunt him like regular, but Charley will have the big job. Every time the pig stands still when he ought to be moving, Charley you give him a little hit with this switch. And every time he plants his rump on the ground when he should be sniffing birds, you hit him a real big hit. Pretty soon, that switch is gonna put fear into him and he'll stop his fooling around."

Charley took hold of the switch and gave a quick snap at a make believe pig.

"Ha!" he said. Then he hit the make believe pig even harder. You could see he was going to enjoy his part of the training. Most of the time Charley was on the other end in the switching business.

We moved out into the field with Homer frisking

behind the hound. He was like a perky shadow for a while, following the hound's point every time. Charley was trailing as close as he could, waiting for Homer to slip up one time. But he didn't do it.

Then after about an hour is when it happened. Homer got tired of chasing the hound and decided to sit down and watch. That's what Charley had been waiting for. A sneaky grin popped on his face and he snuck up on the little pig and snapped him a good one on the ham.

The little pig squealed, jumped about a foot in the air, and started his feet treading air, all at the same time. He hit the ground and headed straight for me. Whatever had happened to him, he didn't want any more of it. All he wanted was a safe place to hide. I knelt down and gave him a hug to comfort him. Then both of us turned and glared at Charley.

"The pig did just what I thought he'd do, Pinch," Dad said. "He ran straight to you. That's why I didn't want you doing the switching. Next time he'll think twice about loafing when he should be working. It's going to take a couple more times, though, 'cause a young pig is about as good a forgetter as a young boy. But he won't be mad at you or me, Son. He's gonna be mad at Charley. Most of the time Charley won't be out in the field with him anyway." I looked over at Charley but he didn't seem to be too concerned about what the pig thought of him, long as he could be the one doing the switching a few more times.

Charley poured his heart into his job after that. He

did so good a job at switching that Homer decided moving was better than sitting. Homer took to stopping, peeking to wherever Charley was, then thinking better of it and getting back to work. Charley was getting to use the switch so seldom he wasn't having any fun, so one day he went home and didn't come back.

After about a week Homer was doing so good, it was hard to tell which was the hound and which was the pig. When the hound froze, Homer did the same. It was something to see, the two of them working together like that. I tell you, pig training beats pig selling every time. I never had so much fun in my life as when I was in the field with that pig. He was a smart little rascal and anybody could see he was partial to me over Dad.

"Pinch, we got us a winner. We got only one more thing to do. I want to see that pig in action by himself."

That afternoon Dad set a bird trap in the field and the next morning there was a killdeer in it.

"It's a perfect day, Son. The fields are wet from the rain last night. The scent of everything is so heavy I could almost do some tracking myself. Now, Pinch, here's what I want you to do. Tie a piece of strong string on this bird's foot and then stake him out in the middle of the field somewhere. We are going to let Homer practice on the real thing."

And that's how we spent the morning, walking that wet field until my shoes and pants legs were solid water. No matter which way we approached the bird or how many times we moved it to a new spot, Homer sniffed it out and held a point. Dad helped him out a little at first, holding up Homer's nose higher and giving his backside a poke so that it would stand up straighter. After a while Homer was doing pretty good all by himself. And he was enjoying himself filling up on apples.

On the way home Dad was a joyous man. "He's a perfect tracker, Pinch. He keeps his nose to the ground all the time. I've seen pigs tracking when they looked like they were chasing butterflies. They would get where they were going, all right, 'cause they were following the wind with their noses. But the wind pushes the scent every which way. Homer follows the scent right on the ground and he's the best I ever seen at doing it. We're doing a good job, Pinch."

The two of us were doing it, me and Dad. We were turning a little pig into something to be proud of. He was coming out a hunting pig, all right. It showed on him more every day. He was born with that nose, but we were showing him how to use it. I forgot all about how I'd wanted to fatten Homer for selling. It seemed like I'd been wanting to be a trainer of hunting pigs for as long as I could remember. My dad was the best in the business and he was teaching me everything he knew. I was learning fast. Someday it was going to be me that was the best in the business. Right now it was him, but I was catching up.

❦ 8 ❦

The Bad Luck Pouch

DAD OR I took Homer out in the fields every day, and he got a big kick out of it. It wasn't too long before Homer was better at pointing birds than any hound dog I ever heard about. You probably don't believe that, but I've got better things to do than tell lies I can get caught at. You had to see that pig in action to really appreciate him. When he's slopping around home, he's just a plain old black and white pig. But when he gets out into the fields with a bunch of birds, all of a sudden he's a panther. His nose is poked out front drawing in scent like he was sniffing perfume. He moves his feet so careful you'd think he was walking on broken glass.

No matter how you look at it, a pig is still a pig, and Homer looks silly out there stalking birds. But the thing is he's so good at it, after a while you forget he should be rooting turnips or doing something else more piglike.

Homer grew to be a lean pig with a long snout, just like Dad hoped he would. He was mostly white, but he had black feet and a black saucer-sized spot sitting on top of him like a midget saddle. Homer never took to riding little kids on his back like some pigs do. All he wanted to do was eat and sleep and hunt birds.

The first time Mr. John Barrow saw Homer at work in a field, we were stirring up killdeer in the cow pasture that belongs to the IC Railroad. That man just sat up in a tree and watched, being so quiet about it I didn't know he was there. After me and Homer had stirred up just about all the killdeer in the cow pasture, he jumped down from his tree hiding place and came flapping his bat wings across the pasture. He was trying his hardest to grin and look pleasant, but it just wasn't in him to do it.

"Good morning, Pinch," he said, and his friendly tone put me on my guard. "That pig is acting mighty funny, Pinch. You don't suppose he's sick or something?"

Well, I knew for sure there was nothing sick about Homer. Why, he just don't get sick. Once when he was littler he swallowed a whole shoe, nails and all, and afterwards he seemed pretty happy about it. Except there was a shoelace hanging out the side of his mouth making him look kind of foolish.

"I been watching you, Pinch, and I'm afraid for you, carrying on with a sick pig." Mr. John Barrow was in the habit of scratching sometimes, and he stood there kneading his scrawny chest, making me want him to keep his distance.

"Nothing wrong with Homer," I told him.

"I tell you what I'll do," he said. "I'll borrow that piece of old rope you got there, and I'll git rid of him for you. Don't guess you knew it, but there's places you can take sick pigs to be disposed of. And they don't charge you too much." He stuck out his hand to take the rope, but I wasn't about to give it to him. So he went on talking like he didn't *have* to have the rope.

"Mr. John Barrow, you got a bird-hunting pig yet for this year's contest?"

"Oh, Pinch, I got plenty of 'em. All of 'em winners. Son, you got any money with you? If you don't I'll even pay whatever it costs to git rid of this pig. I'll do it jist to show how strong I feel about you associating yourself with a sickly pig."

"Mr. John Barrow, this pig is as well as you or me and maybe weller. Besides, he's my friend and I don't plan on getting rid of him, so good-bye." And I started walking off on him. But he hippety-hopped on his skinny old bat legs until he got in front of me, and he moved in close. The closer he got, the more I feared his scratching 'cause he was getting within bedbug jumping distance.

Another thing that bothered me was the bad luck pouch hanging from around his waist. There were folks who said that pouch caused the fishing to go bad when Mr. John Barrow was around. It was a soft leather bag about the size of my fist. Nobody knew what he kept in it. Some said it was a voodoo charm like a dried up cat's eyeball. But I was betting on it having money value, 'cause that's the way Mr. John Barrow's mind runs. Something like a solid gold false tooth, or maybe a pearl as big as a banty egg. Some said he lived with that pouch days and slept with it nights. And anybody who dared ask him about it, he'd just walk away and wouldn't say a word to that fellow for as long as a week. He just wasn't telling what was in his pouch. Even if it was a thousand dollars, which it wasn't. He didn't need a thousand dollars anyway. Mr. John Barrow had all he could have wanted. He had a house he got from his paw and the roof didn't leak too bad. He had twenty acres of land and only about half of it was swamp. He had more scrawny chickens than you could count. And he had a piece of mule to get his field work done. Nobody needed much more than that.

But he sure was being persistent about wanting Homer. "Pinch, now why don't you sell me that scrawny pig and save yourself a lot of trouble? You jist might be catching what he has. Illness can be painful, you know. It can twist you up in knots and it can boil your blood and it can make your head wind and unwind like it was ready to twist right off." He was squirming and wiggling his skinny self around to make sure I got what he was saying. "Jist suppose you caught something bad and brought it home to your maw and paw? Now I could offer you a quarter for that sickly pig. You think what you could do with a whole quarter?" But he wasn't moving his hand toward his pocket. He just leaned over and scratched his ankle. I kept on heading for home.

"Stop now, Pinch. I wasn't going to say anything about this to a living soul, but son, you know that pig is partly mine. It was my chickens you traded for that pig, Pinch. Now you remember that, don't you?"

But that was getting to be an old trick, and it wasn't going to help him this time. I kept walking.

"Wait now, son. Don't run off in a hurry," he said in his whiney voice and grabbed at me like he was going to hold fast to me if he had to. "What would you say to a great big silver dollar for that poor old sickly pig? I think that's a mighty fine offer and about the best I can do."

Right then I learned something plenty of folks had been waiting to find out, 'cause Mr. John Barrow stopped his scratching and put his hand on top of that leather pouch hanging from his waist.

It was a money pouch, that's what it was!

"Mr. John Barrow, how many silver dollars you got in that pouch?"

"What!" He turned on me so sudden I thought I was going to get a hit in the head. That's when I remembered he didn't take kindly to questions about his pouch. He straightened up and started clutching tight onto it like he thought I might try to grab it away from him.

"You jist keep your skinny old pig!" he yelled at me.

"He's on death's door, that's for sure. I don't need him."

He spun around and moved off, bat wings flapping in the air. And that ended it. But when I turned to head for my house I saw something near a tree across the road. It was Billy Sweet standing in the shadows. He had been watching everything that happened and it looked like he was as keen on Homer as Mr. John Barrow was. He didn't say anything. He just stood near the tree watching and smiling.

Next morning trouble started. Billy and Henry Sweet knocked on the door and told my dad they had come for their pig, which they had traded fair and square for a fine, healthy mule. And it wasn't any of their business what Pinch had gone and done with the mule. Well, that told you for sure that the Sweets didn't have a pig for this year's hunting pig contest either. Dad wasn't about to turn Homer loose and he told them to get about their business, if they had any.

"We got business, all right, Mr. Grimball." But they didn't say what the business was. They left. It wasn't until long after they were gone that I noticed my treasure box was missing off the porch where I kept it. Jean Laffite, my genuine pirate skull, was inside the missing box.

9

The Pig Parade

WE FOUND OUT about the Sweets' business later that night. It was pig stealing. There was a screeching out in the back yard and Dad grabbed his shotgun and light and went running. I was ready for bed but I pulled on a pair of pants and raced out after him. He was standing out by the pig pen, and his shotgun was trained on Billy Sweet's nose. Billy was silly-talking.

"I, ah, you, ah, I'll tell you, ah, please . . ."

Billy was holding onto a piece of rope and a pig was on the other end.

"Billy Sweet, you march that pig back to its rightful pen," Dad said. "Then we will go see Sheriff Tony about this."

But when we got him back to Homer's pen, there was a sleepy pig inside. Dad turned the light on both pigs and you couldn't tell them apart. They were like brothers. Both were white and both were kind of skinny and both had a black saddle spot and black feet. It didn't take long to figure out what Billy Sweet was up to. He was trading some dumb look-alike pig for our smart one. Then he would use Homer to win the hunting pig contest.

"Billy Sweet, which one of these pigs is mine, and which one is somebody else's, and you better be quick about telling me if you don't want to hear shotgun noises."

"Mr. Grimball, you got me dead to rights. I scrounged up a yard pig and put him in Homer's pen. Then I was going to take Homer here and we would go for a walk." Dad's teeth were showing and the anger was boiling. Billy saw it coming and hopped back from him. "Now, Mr. Grimball, hold on. I'm here looking after your own interest. I know you like pigs, and you can see that the pig I left over there in the pen is a better looking pig than the one I got here. So I thought I would trade you the good pig for the bad pig."

I was all for getting Homer back into his pen where he could get some sleep. I gave him a push and my hand came away greasy. Under the light it looked like soot.

"Homer's got soot all over him, Dad." He came over and took a look. Then he rubbed his fingers on the saddle spot and his fingers came away black. He looked at those fingers for a minute and then walked over and took a close look at the sleepy pig in the pen and did some rubbing on *his* back.

"Billy Sweet, this funny business is gonna stop right now." He poked the shotgun a little closer to Billy's nose. "That's my pig in the pen. This dirty pig here belongs to you or somebody. Now where did you get the twin of my pig Homer?"

"You right, Mr. Grimball. I was just playing fun.

But these ain't twin pigs," he said, bending over and stroking his pig. "Why, look a here, Henry must've used a little boot polish on this one to spot him up and make him look a little prettier. Henry must've thought you would like it better if the pig didn't look his usual pale color." His hand was black with boot polish.

Dad wasn't pleased by all of this and he was yelling to let Billy know about it.

"I tell you Billy Sweet, you better take your shoe polishy pig and get away from here. Pig stealing is against the law. And pig swapping is too. Don't you ever try something like this on me again, 'cause next time it won't be words that'll be chasing you out. It'll be two barrels of double ought buckshot that'll be doing it. Now, get on home and start training that silly pig, cause that's your only chance of winning second prize in the hunting pig contest. You got no chance at all of winning first prize, 'cause Homer's gonna take that. Now move!" He said it like he hoped that Billy wouldn't do it and he could shoot him where he stood. But Billy didn't give him the chance.

You would think that the foolishness would stop after that but next morning there was a banging on the front door and Mr. John Barrow was standing out there looking mighty grim.

"Pinch, I told you that pig was going to cause you trouble. You should've took that quarter I offered you and then it would've been all over."

"Mr. John Barrow, what are you talking about?"

"That sick pig of yours was rooting in my vegetable

patch. And if that wasn't enough, when I tried chasing him out he jumped me. I had to shoot him in self-defense. So you can come over and haul his carcass off my property. I don't want no sick pig spreading germs on my place."

I felt sick. I never thought he'd kill my Homer. No man could be that mean. Dad and I had raised that pig from a pup. I only had one human friend I liked better than Homer. Mr. John Barrow was going to get it for this! I balled up both my fists and gritted my teeth and kicked him square in the shin.

"Help, boy! Don't be like that!" He started hopping around on one leg. "Now you come on and move that pig. I'll give you a hand hauling him as far as the road."

I tell you, I was breathing fire! I never knew a pig like Homer before. I never would again. And all because of a skinny, mean, ornery, dirty, stingy, ugly, broken-down old man who didn't like pigs and pigs didn't like him. He limped off, favoring the leg I didn't get to kick. I was so mad I could have cried, but I wasn't going to do it. I just stood there and swallowed hard. If Homer was gone, there wasn't anything else to do.

Then it hit me. What if that pig was only a little bit hurt and needed help bad!

I never ran so fast in my whole life! Mr. John Barrow heard me coming and he jumped off the road to get out of the way, flinging his arms up to protect himself. But I passed him by like a lightning flash and didn't slow down until I had got to the barbed wire that was around his vegetable garden. Even from there though, I could see it was too late.

What was left of Homer was lying in a furrow, mighty still and cold looking. He was the only bird-hunting pig I ever had, and he would never hunt another bird again. He looked strange and pitiful lying there. In fact, the closer I got to him, the stranger he looked. I walked up slow, and a funny feeling kept growing on me every step.

There was something different about that pig. I didn't know what it was, but it didn't set right.

Then I knew it! That wasn't Homer lying there at all! It was a pig that looked like him all right. But this here pig surely wasn't my hunting pig. It didn't look smart enough, for one thing. And its nose was too small for sniffing proper. I was ready to whoop for joy when Mr. John Barrow ducked under the barbed wire and yelled at me, "All right now, you git him out of here. I don't want no buzzards flying in my yard to git at no dead, sickly pig."

I turned around and grinned at him, and that kind of shook him.

"Mr. John Barrow, this isn't my pig. This is some strange pig. You got a pig problem all your own. And you won't get any help from me hauling it out of here."

"You sure, Pinch?" He was as surprised as he could be. But he didn't stay surprised for long. He grabbed hold of one of the hind legs and pulled it about an inch toward his house. "Well, in that case, I guess it belongs to whoever has it. I think I jist came into more ham and pork chops than I ever expected this time of year. Beats eating chicken, Pinch."

I'd had enough of Mr. John Barrow for one day and I turned my back on him without even a good-bye and stomped off toward the fence. But I hadn't gone ten feet when he hollered so loud I jumped around quick.

"Pinch, look a here!" He was pointing to a spot at the far end of the garden. There was another live pig sitting over there in the shade. It was a big one, bigger than the one he had filled full of buckshot.

"And look a there!" I looked over by the house and there were two more pigs coming round the corner. And behind them came two more. It was a marching parade of pigs. They were coming up out of the ground, from behind the bushes, and everywhere.

"Mr. John Barrow, it looks like there must have been another accident out on the highway." The highway is a heavy traveled dirt road running through the woods about a quarter mile from his house. Last summer a truck loaded with chicken coops had thrown a wheel and scattered chickens like cotton balls. We were up to our knees in Leghorns for a week while they roamed around looking for a worm or a handout. People were cornering them, or netting them, or just giving them a swat with a two-by-four. That was how Mr. John Barrow got his start in the chicken-raising business. And you could tell that now he was thinking about adding pigs to his line of goods.

"Pinch," he said, glowing like a light bulb, "this is a chance of a lifetime. Why, those pigs must be worth at least a dollar apiece. You and me could team up and catch 'em all! Son, why probably nobody else even knows they're loose yet. Why there might be fifty pigs running loose out there! You could use five dollars or so this time of year, couldn't you?"

To tell the truth I was thinking in that direction myself. With all that pig money, my fortune would be made for sure. I didn't have any real liking for taking on Mr. John Barrow as a partner, 'cause his arithmetic wasn't too good. Every time he added up something, it was going to come out in his favor. But two *could* catch pigs better than one.

"Mr. John Barrow, those pigs are worth plenty more than a dollar apiece, and if I help you we're equal partners, fifty-fifty."

"I'll agree to that, Pinch. You're jist about the best businessman I ever came across. Your paw sure trained you good in bargaining. Now, why don't you go on home and git that piece of rope I saw you with the other day. We're going to need it if we're going to git started making our fortunes."

❦ 10 ❧

Catching Pigs

For the rest of the day I saw more of pigs than I really cared to. I tackled them and Indian wrestled them and flopped around in the mud with them and got bit and kicked by them. One even kissed me, though I don't know if that was its intention. And if another old sow had been a bit quicker I might have got my ear chewed off, but I outsmarted her and grabbed a handful of bristle and bit her ear first. And only about a minute after that, a giant red one outdodged me when I was running low to tackle him, and I butted my head onto an oak tree that wouldn't give an inch. I was knocked clear out of my head for I don't know how long, but Mr. John Barrow told me later I did some of my best pig catching then.

When we were done we had caught six whole pigs exactly and stored them in the mule pen and my fortune was made! The rest of those pigs had scattered so far it would be nighttime before we could get hold of even one more. So we decided to quit. It had been a hard day's work and I was tired from it. Even if Mr. John Barrow pulled every crafty trick in the book, we had a solid agreement. My share of the pig money was bound to be considerable, and it was nice resting and thinking about it. I was leaning on the mule pen before deciding to go home when I heard something that sounded familiar mixed in with all those pig noises. I hopped up on the rails to take a good look, and there was Homer in with all those *common* pigs. He was looking up at me and "roonking" away for me to get him out of there.

"Mr. John Barrow!" I yelled.

"Pinch, I'm too tired to talk right now," he said. He was just laying on the ground by the water trough where the overflow from the pump made the ground damp and cool.

"Mr. John Barrow, you got my Homer in this pen! You sneaked off and caught him by yourself and put him in this mule pen! Now get him out of here!" I might have known a man like him wouldn't hesitate pulling a sneaky trick like that.

"Now, Pinch, if your pig is in there we can talk about it. I told you we would split fifty-fifty, and I'll jist make him a part of your share."

"But we were going to split on the wild pigs. Homer is a *tame* pig. You know yourself, he's a genuine hunting pig!" I didn't hold back on the yelling, 'cause I wanted him to know I meant it. All day long is too long to have to spend with a man like him. It rubs you raw.

"Well, Pinch, if you feel that strong about it I'll do it," he said, and gave his belly a scratch. "But I'm absolutely sure your pig ain't in there to start with. So we'll jist have to consider this *strange* pig I'm giving you is part of whatever you jist possibly might have coming if I ever git to sell the rest of these pigs." We fiddled and shuffled pigs around until we got Homer up front and then we hauled him out of there, fighting off those common pigs from every direction. Homer was a mighty happy pig. He gave me a grunt or two and then started hopping around the yard like a butterfly, glad to be free again. Next thing I knew he was sniffing around the porcupine's box on the front porch and it was the worst idea he ever had. That porcupine slapped Homer square in the nose with his tail and Homer let out the loudest yell I ever heard a pig make. Before I had a chance to get close to him he was out of the yard and kicking up dust on the road. By the time I got home, he was in his pen and Dad was already outside with pliers in his hands.

"We got to get those quills out quick, Pinch. You leave them in long and they will work their way right inside."

Homer wasn't any too happy about what happened next. Porcupine quills have barbs like thistles and they hurt coming out even more than going in. But he was pretty brave about it and didn't do too much grunting and snorting. I held him tight while Dad pulled them out. Then I sat with that poor pig until dark. We didn't talk or anything, 'cause he wasn't feeling so good. But I knew he'd want company, 'cause I remember the time I fell out of the fig tree and broke my leg. Mom would come sit on the edge of the bed and not do anything, but her just being there made me feel good.

❦ 11 ❧

Selling Pigs

I GAVE the pig market a day or two to get sprightly and then me and Charley went back to check up on how Mr. John Barrow was doing with those pigs. Homer came with us as far as the gate but he wouldn't go any farther. When we got there, the mule pen only had a mule in it. There wasn't a single pig in sight. Mr. John Barrow heard me yelling and stomping and came outside to see what was the matter.

"Mr. John Barrow, where are all our pigs?"

He was a pitiful sight to see. His head was drooped low and his big feet were shuffling along in the dust. He gave Charley and me a sorrowful look like maybe he was suffering from a boil on his backside.

"I'm afraid I got some bad news for you, Pinch. I'm really and truly sorry now, but them pigs we caught broke loose last night and ate up about two dozen of my chickens. It was all I could do to recatch them all by myself alone. And, of course, I can't afford to lose that kind of money on dead chickens. I had to sell them pigs quick jist to keep me from going bankrupt or something. And I really only sold what was truly mine, since I did all the catching."

Now, that did it! He was cheating me out of my pig money and trying to make me feel it was the only thing he could have done. My fists were balled up and I was snorting like a bull.

"But half of that pig money is mine! You know that! You promised if I helped half would be mine. Look how I skinned my knee when I dove at that black one. And I still got a bump on my head from where I hit that oak chasing the big red one. You can't change everything now, when all the work is done!"

Mr. John Barrow kept shuffling his feet around and looking up in the sky to see if it was going to rain and looking down at those big feet to see if they were still there and sneaking a look at Charley to see if it was going to be two against one. He was looking just about everywhere except straight at me.

"You're absolutely right, Pinch," he finally answered. He said it so sincere, you'd have thought he was talking to the preacher. "And I tell you, young fellow, if it was up to me, I sure would give you at least one of them pigs if they was still here. I'd even give you that black one, and he was the biggest of them all." He was looking at me kind of sideways now and he was shaking his head from side to side and his arms were waving out in front of him. He was like a swamp flower waving in the breeze. All of that was supposed to mean that if I didn't believe every word he said it would break his heart. "But it ain't up to me no more. They're sold now, and the damage done to my chickens is made up for. A man jist can't go bankrupt 'cause of a bunch of pigs, now, can he?"

"Mr. John Barrow, you owe me, and you're going to pay. I'm going to get Sheriff Tony to come out here and he's going to put handcuffs on you. You'll be in jail the rest of your mean life!"

Believe me, I was learning my lesson from this. When you bargain with Mr. John Barrow you better get it all down in writing and have it checked over by a city lawyer. Otherwise you're going to come out short every time.

"You just give me my piece of rope and I'll get away from this place."

He put his hands behind him like he was holding my rope in his hands, which he wasn't. "Oh, I'm sorry about that too, Pinch. Two dozen chickens is worth a lot more than a few skinny pigs. I sold that rope for a quarter so as to make up some of the difference. I'm truly sorry about that, son. But you can git yourself another piece of rope from somewhere if you ever need it. I got to go now, Pinch, but I do want to thank you for all your help and all that."

Well, that did it! I picked up a broken tree branch and swung it at his raggedy head, but I was so mad I missed. Charley got himself a rock and was coming at him from the other side. Mr. John Barrow pulled his skinny shoulders up around his ears like a turtle and lit out. About two long-legged hops and he was up his front steps, on his porch, and in his house, hiding behind the screen door for protection.

Safe inside, he didn't seem to mind talking about it.

"Don't be like that, boys," he said. "Pinch, we sure had a good time catching them pigs, didn't we?"

My ears were pounding, I was so mad. I was getting ready to kick a hole in his screen door so the mosquitoes would feast on him tonight, but I didn't get to do it. All of a sudden he started whooping and slammed the door against me and rushed out into the yard. Charley had opened his chicken yard gate and was shooing every one of them scrawny chickens out into the open. It was such a good idea, I wish I'd thought of it myself.

We left while Mr. Barrow was running around in circles with a chicken under each arm and looking like he was wishing he had about six more arms to catch chickens with.

Charley and me walked home feeling pretty good about it. I didn't go after Sheriff Tony like I said I would, 'cause Mr. John Barrow sold him chickens sometimes and he might not see it our way. But I did tell my dad about how Mr. John Barrow sold those pigs out from under me and Dad said if I wanted to fool around doing business with a man like that, I had to expect to get caught short once in a while. That didn't help much.

Mr. John Barrow and I kept out of each other's way for a while after that, but Four Corners never got any prizes for bigness and two days later we came head to head in front of Mr. Tony's store.

"Hi, Pinch." He kicked up a little dirt and stood

there with his hands in his pockets. I didn't have anything to say to him.

"Pinch?"

"What?"

"Ain't you going to talk to me?" He kicked up some more dirt. He wasn't looking at me exactly, but more at the dirt.

"Pinch, about them pigs you and me caught together."

"What about them."

"Well, they really did git at my chickens, Pinch. I told you the truth. I sold them at the Farmer's Market to help cut down my losses."

"I know you did. I checked up on you."

"You don't mind too much, do you, Pinch?"

"I was set to make my fortune, Mr. John Barrow."

"Son, you wouldn't want to make your fortune by me going broke, now would you?"

I didn't have anything to say to that. He was looking at me now, right in the eyes, and when he looks at you hard, it's not too easy looking back at him.

"Pinch, you and me friends or not?"

I hadn't thought much about it. It was fun doing things with him. Needed to keep a close eye on him when money was a part of whatever you were doing but except for that I guess we were almost as much friends as me and Charley. He was sticking his old skinny hand out in front of him, and so I shook it and we smiled at each other kind of sickly and I stopped thinking mean thoughts about him.

🌿 12 🌿

The Stranger

HOMER turned out to be a summer pig. Didn't take us long to find out once the weather began to get cool. He slept outside in his pen like all the other pigs and his long, skinny frame was more suited to hunting than to keeping him warm. If he'd of had some meat on him, maybe it would've been different. Some of the bad things might not have happened. But he didn't. And they did.

It got so cold out there, even that old pig's water pail froze solid nights. After supper his head would droop and he would walk a slow pace to the back porch. There he'd look up at the door closing to hide the kitchen light and heat from him. Then, instead of going back to his pen, he'd curl under the back porch steps where I'd thrown a few sacks. He'd twist into a ball the way a scared doodle bug does. He'd try his best to go to sleep. But nobody could sleep out on such a freezing night, with wind whistling and cold creeping so deep it starts feeling like heat. I couldn't sleep out like that. I tried it once. And neither could old Homer.

What I really wanted to do was sneak him inside with me at night, but Mom and Dad wouldn't be too pleased about that. I don't fool around much where Dad is concerned. He doesn't care for it and has his ways of letting me know. My backside is still sore just remembering the licking I got when all I did was leave a dead bird in the hall closet a day or so too long. But after about a week of Homer freezing solid nights and looking at me mornings as though I was as mean as he was frozen, I sneaked him through my bedroom window one night. Both of us were pleased.

When Dad and Mom woke up the next morning he was gone. I had got him out in time. But not all of him.

"We've got to give this room an airing," Mom said. "There's an animal smell about it. Have you got another bird hidden in here somewhere?"

"No, sir, Mom!"

"You don't have some kind of creature bigger than an old bird, do you now?" She began poking around.

"No, sir, Mom. For sure not. There's nothing in this room but us. Unless you count a few little spiders here and there." I thought I'd poke some fun and turn her mind away, 'cause I could smell that pig too, but Mom had a hard way about her. She stuck to her ideas like grits sticks to an old iron pot.

But finally she went away, and I got up and dressed and picked pig bristles out of the bed. After breakfast, I took Homer for a walk. He was hard to live with that day, scampering every which way. He knew we had put one over on old Mom, and I felt pretty good about it myself, even though I was sure I was risking more than he was. But it didn't turn out to be that way.

A couple of things happened after that. Mom made Dad nail wood slats across the outside of my bedroom window just in case I might get ideas about letting the pig in my room.

"We're doing it to keep night creatures out, Pinch," Mom said.

That kept Homer out in the cold a night or two. But then I got me a smart idea, and when Mom and Dad went visiting and stayed away from the house a whole day, I set to it. I had figured out a way for Homer to get in the house without coming through the window, and while they were away I fixed it.

Our house sits about three feet off the ground on brick pillars. That helps make things cooler in the summer and keeps some of the ground crawling bugs, and snakes too, out where they belong. To make short telling of a job that took me all day long, I loosened some boards in the floor under my bed and made a trapdoor. Then I taught Homer to come through, using kitchen scraps to get him in, and nudging him out gentle when I wanted him to be gone.

When we got to where he was good at it, I called a quit to practicing and put a brick on the boards to keep him out. Then that night when all of us were in bed I took off the brick and whistled and he came hopping in, first his nose, then all of him. He was a mighty pleased looking pig.

But all that work caused my downfall, 'cause I slept so sound that when Mom came into my room in the morning to wake me up, the first one to wake up was the pig.

It was Mom's first yell that woke me up. And I stayed awake, 'cause she was using strong language to express her feelings. I never heard Mom get so upset about a pig before.

"Get that dirty old pig out of my clean house!" she hollered, and I knew she really meant it. She skittered out of my room long enough to get hold of a broom, and she came back with a weapon Homer had respect for. He skidded under the bed, and for a minute I thought he'd find a way to open the trapdoor and save himself a licking. Then I started praying he wouldn't, 'cause if he found a way out from under the bed, I'd really be a gonner. That dead bird licking wouldn't half stand up to what I'd get.

But Homer didn't make it. Mom's broom poked him a good one in the ribs and out into the open where she could get a clean lick at him as he scooted toward the door. And even though he was just a gray blur crossing from the bed to the door, old Mom got in one good lick across his backside that moved him out the room ten miles an hour faster. But that was her last lick. He scurried out the door and into the kitchen.

For a minute I thought his troubles were over and he was safe, but this just wasn't his day. That old pig's idea to *go out* the back door and Dad's idea to *come in* the back door came at the same split second. That's when the bad luck spread, 'cause Dad was bringing in the morning milk pail, and it was full to the brim.

CREEKSIDE ELEMENTARY SCHOOL
MORENO VALLEY UNIFIED SCHOOL DISTRICT

There's no sense in trying to figure out exactly who hit what first, but by the time the pail came down, there was milk dripping from the ceiling, milk sizzling on the hot stove, milk drenching Dad's clothes and soaking him clean to the underwear. The floor was an awful mess, and old Homer got his share too, but it didn't even slow him down.

Mom thought I'd done wrong and she let me know it as certain as she had that old pig. Dad and the kitchen both smelled sour for a week, even though I cleaned up the kitchen as best I knew how. For about three days Dad didn't take to me too well. In fact, he made sure to keep out of my way. He never was any too keen about bathing more than necessary in wintertime.

"I gave up a lot of real hunting to train that pig. And all the thanks I get is a dousing with a bucket of milk. Pinch, like your mom says, you keep that pig out of this house. And what's more, I don't care to have anything to do with him from here on. He's your problem. You take care of him. I'm out of the hunting pig business."

But everything considered, I didn't think I had it too bad until suppertime when Mom looked at me across the supper table and said, "I sold your pig to a stranger who passed by about an hour ago. He said he'd take good care of him."

I looked at her and she looked at me, and I didn't know what to say. I wasn't hungry any more. I didn't care if I left the table or not. I just sat.

But Dad didn't just sit. First he stared at her, his

mouth open and a spoonful of gravy stuck in the air halfway between his plate and his face. Then he put the spoon down hard, gravy popping every which way, and started yelling.

"Victoria Grimball, that was my pig you sold. I bought him off of Pinch and I helped the boy with the training. No matter how much you got for him from the stranger, it don't make up for all the hours I put in training the boy and the pig." He stopped his yelling then, 'cause Mom was staring right back at him harder than he was yelling. He picked up his spoon again and looked at it. After a while he got tired looking at the spoon.

"How much did you get for the pig?" he asked.

"Ten dollars," she said and took the money out of her apron pocket and laid it down on the table in front of him.

He looked at it. It was a real ten dollar bill.

"We could have done better," he said. But ten dollars was enough to stop his yelling. He picked it up and put it in his pocket.

Then both of them turned and looked at me, but I didn't have anything to say to them. Dad might have helped train him, but it was my pig that Mom gave away and they both knew it. There weren't any more words after that, and we all went to bed.

The trouble is boys don't have enough friends. I've been a boy all my life and I've got only one friend unless you count Mr. John Barrow. Then along came Homer and it was different. Having two friends is better than having only one, no matter how good that one friend is. Homer listened when I wanted to talk. He walked in the woods with me when I felt like walking. And I did the same for him. It hurts, him not being here. It hurts too much even to tell Charley about it. I'm going to miss that pig. I don't want to cry, but I might have to. Maybe I have to.

❧ 13 ❧

The Trapdoor

Mom came by once or twice in the middle of the night and poked her head in my room. There wasn't any old pig in there, and nobody ought to have known that better than her. Maybe it was she wasn't sleeping so well. That happened to her sometimes. I know for sure I didn't sleep too well.

Next morning I felt mighty lonely, and it stayed that way for a while. I sure did miss that old pig. I had pancakes for breakfast almost every morning that week, so I knew Mom had let it all pass from her mind and wasn't staying mad at me. She usually didn't. And Dad forgot all about that extra bath after about a week, and he took me with him once or twice when he ran his trapping lines. And he began talking to me again about things that were bothering him like he always used to do.

"The icy weather's doing its work on the chimney, Pinch. There's a chunk of mortar big as my finger missing from one place. That chimney's so old, we're risking fire every time we light up kindling in the grate. Next summer I'm going to take it down, brick by brick, and build it up again with my own hands. That way I'll know it's O.K." He looked over at me. "Maybe you could help me do it, Pinch."

Later that day I went to see Mr. John Barrow to tell him about what happened to Homer. He hadn't heard about it, and it really bothered him.

"That was a mighty fine hunting pig to git sold to a stranger," he said. He had his shotgun with him and we walked through the field behind his house looking for rabbit droppings. "I tell you one thing, son. A pig's no good at traveling. Pigs like to settle down in one place. The stranger will find that out soon enough. Pinch, you think he knew he got a real hunting pig? Otherwise, he might butcher him for meat and fat."

Well, I didn't want to hear that!

"Mr. John Barrow, all you are doing is making me feel worse." I wasn't interested in finding rabbits anymore.

"I'm sorry about that, Pinch. But no use fooling yourself that a thing ain't so. That's what my paw always used to say. Homer's gone, whether he's out in the field hunting with somebody else or in somebody's cooking pot, he's still gone. Ain't much chance you'll ever see him again. That's all I'm saying, Pinch. I sure don't want to make you feel any badder than you do. I'm doing my best to cheer you up, son."

But he wasn't making too good a job of it.

If it was cold when Homer was around, it got colder after he was gone. For about a week we had one granddaddy of a cold spell, with me chopping a ton of wood to keep the fireplace lit days and most of the night. It was go-to-school and chop-wood, go-to-school and chop-wood. Nothing but that. I'd be swinging that ax and wondering how Homer was doing. After a while I almost gave up ever seeing him again. Anything could have happened to him. The stranger might have killed him with meanness. Old Homer could have froze to death in that granddaddy cold spell. I knew a boy who lost a pup in it, and two of our chickens had froze stiff. So I about called it quits on that old pig.

Then came one cold night when Homer saved my life.

I was sleeping sound. Then all of a sudden I woke up. It wasn't light yet but it had the feel of early morning and there were shadows dancing on the walls. I can usually tell when morning is near 'cause by then the fire in the grate has died down and my room is ice cold. But it wasn't cold. It was warm, and worse still, I was having trouble breathing. I started tossing in bed, and when I drew air in it bit sharp and I nearly died of coughing.

It was smoke! I sat up fast. Smoke was billowing in the room. The wall by the fireplace was blazing and there was flame running across the floor between the fireplace and the door. The old chimney wasn't lasting until next summer. It was going to burn the house to the ground this very night! I could hear Dad and Mom on the other side of my door, but there wasn't any way for them to get through. I backed off from the heat and moved over to the window but it wouldn't budge. Those wood slats that Dad had nailed on to keep the pig out were keeping me in. Dad had run outside and was at the window. He yelled for me to get back and rammed a pole through the glass. Smoke drained out while we yelled back and forth through the slats. Mom was out there in the morning light, safe. But I wasn't. Flames covered the whole wall and the heat parched my face and arms. I was in the middle of a hot frying pan and I had to find a way past the flames without sizzling like bacon. Last time I had to worry about getting out of this room was the night Homer slept in the bed with me.

The trapdoor!

I scooted under the bed so fast I picked up splinters on one side and the bedsprings nearly tore the pajama pants off me on the other. I flung those boards open and dropped to the ground and crawled through cobwebs and whatever to get out from under the house. I came out in back and stood up quick and pulled in fresh air. Then I ran around to the side and the first thing I saw was Dad swinging the wood ax at those window bars with every bit of his strength. By then yellow flames were crackling out the window at him, stroke for stroke.

Mom saw me first, and she grabbed me and pulled me close. She shouted to Dad but he didn't hear. He chopped at that window like his very soul depended on it, and the ax tore through good wood like it was made of cotton. I always knew he was a strong man, but I never knew how strong until that day.

That ax came down again and again in a fury. One swing struck so deep in the sill that half the axhead was buried in the wood. He fought it hard and the handle snapped, throwing him backward on the ground. He was on his knees, heading back for more, when he must have heard Mom screaming 'cause he turned suddenly and saw the two of us standing there.

He stood still for a moment, sweat running down his face. The broken ax handle dropped from his hand. His head sank down on his chest. He walked over slowly and his big, strong hand touched on my shoulder. Then he moved off a ways and sat down on an old log and didn't say a word.

I wanted to go over and tell him about the trapdoor and about how if it hadn't been for me thinking of Homer I'd never have made it. But Mom said it would keep.

❧ 14 ❧

The Pignapping

Next morning Dad and I were scraping up burned wood and starting to rebuild the piece of the house that had burned when Billy Sweet came by and took a look and told my Dad, "Mr. Grimball, I surely didn't wish you this bad luck, but you see what happens when a man keeps a pig what ain't really his." Dad chased him clear to the school house, but he didn't catch him. I didn't even get a chance to ask Billy where was my treasure box and my genuine pirate skull.

We went back to work until Mom brought us out some hot milk coffee. Then we stopped hammering and sawing and took a rest. We talked about the fire and all that happened. I told him if I ever got trapped like that in a fire again I surely wanted it to be him chopping to get me out. He didn't say anything. He just looked at me for a long time. Then he smiled and scratched the top of my head like grown-ups do sometimes when they are happy and are talking to kids.

Later in the morning Mr. John Barrow stopped by. I told him about Billy Sweet's visit and said he better not say anything to Dad about pigs unless he was up on his running.

"I'll take my chances on that, Pinch. Your paw is going to want to hear what I got to say, so you go and call him."

We went and found Dad. He was up a ladder and wasn't too pleased about having to come down to talk to Mr. John Barrow. But he did it anyway.

"Mr. Grimball, I been across the road at the store. Tony says he knows what happened to your pig. A stranger was here yesterday and told him all about it."

"I quit on that pig, John. You want to tell your story, you tell it to Pinch." He started to climb back up the ladder.

"That mean you don't want to know that the Sweet boys got your pig?"

Well, that slowed Dad from his climbing. He climbed back down and stood in front of Mr. John Barrow, hands on hips, like he was going to bite his head off.

"All right, John, let's hear whatever it is you got to say."

"Well, a stranger stopped by Tony's store yesterday and told him two big husky men stopped him on the road about a mile from here and stole his pig away from him. He said they kept calling him a pig stealer and that they were taking the pig away to make sure it got back to its rightful owners. But he told Tony *he* was the rightful owner. He said he was the one what bought the pig from Mrs. Grimball and paid her ten good dollars for it." Mr. John Barrow was having a fine time telling his story 'cause he knew it was a stirring-up kind of story. It was stirring up trouble between my Dad and the Sweets, but Dad wasn't having any of it.

"I tell you, John. Hunting with pigs instead of dogs is a fever. I've had it bad in the past. But I just don't have it right now. I don't care what happens to that pig. If Pinch wants to worry about it, he can. But I don't plan to." And he went back up his ladder.

Well, I sure didn't feel the same way he did. I turned around and headed for Mr. Tony's store as fast as I could.

"Pinch, what you going to do?" Mr. John Barrow was following me so he could be in on the action.

"I'm going to get Sheriff Tony to help me catch those thieving Sweets, that's what I'm going to do."

But when we got there Mr. Tony didn't feel like sheriffing just then. He said he had work to do around the store.

"But I'll get around to it, Pinch. I told that stranger that I'd either get his money or his pig back. And you know I'm a man of my word."

"Well, I don't plan to wait around here while you get your work done. I don't want those Sweets to have Homer one minute longer than necessary. They'll ruin him, they might even butcher him. And I don't want any stranger to have him either. I'll get a hold of ten dollars and buy him back if I have to. I'll even do that work for you in the store if you ever get around to starting it. But right now I'm going to get my pig from those pig-stealing Sweets."

"Son, you take care. Those Sweets are mighty interested in being the ones to win the hunting pig contest this year. And since they don't have a speck of talent between them to train a pig proper, they are going to look to other ways to win."

"Amen to that," said Mr. John Barrow.

I left the store with Mr. John Barrow still following.

"Pinch. I'm gonna help you git your justice. You need some help, don't you? I don't want them Sweets to win the contest any more than you do. If I can't win it, then maybe we will let your dad win it again this year. Son, let's stop off at my house and git my shotgun. That way we'll have a better chance of gitting them Sweets to listen to what you are going to say to them about stealing pigs."

Well, that made some sense. So we did it. Then we decided that it wouldn't be a bad idea to have them outnumbered, so we went to get Charley. But when we got to his house, he wasn't there. His dad said he had heard about the Sweets having Homer, and he was going to see if it was true.

"I told him to stay away from Billy and Henry 'cause they are mean when they get liquored up. He said he'd stay away, Pinch, but that boy's got a mighty curiosity about him. You tell him he ain't back here in one hour, I'm going to give him a licking. I'd chase after him myself, but I got to go to work down at the filling station right this minute."

I was hoping Charley was smart enough not to take on the Sweets all by himself. Mr. John Barrow was thinking the same thing, 'cause he said, "Now don't you worry none, Pinch. We'll rescue Charley, even if they have kidnapped him."

We trotted down the road, and when we got within yelling distance of Henry Sweet's place, we crept up slow and silent. There were more dry twigs on the ground than was reasonable, and Mr. John Barrow's big feet were making them snap like a bunch of baby firecrackers.

"I can't help it," he whispered, "I was born with these here feet."

We stopped and didn't make a sound. Nobody was in the yard and we couldn't hear any talk coming from the house.

"You think they're in there, Pinch?" he whispered.

"Can't hear a sound, but they're in there, all right."

"We better be quiet then, 'cause I wouldn't want them finding out we was here and harming Charley." Then he stepped on a dry branch and it cracked like a rifle and that ended them not knowing somebody was outside. We knelt down and kept an eye on the door. It was quiet as a church on weekdays. Then the door started opening just a little bit and a skinny head poked out.

"Who's out there?" It was Charley, looking a little worried, but no worse for wear.

"Charley! We're here," I yelled at him. But Mr. John Barrow wasn't having any of that.

"Pinch," he said sharply, "you got to let me run things now. This is man's work." Then he put his shotgun to his shoulder like he was ready for the worst.

"Charley," he yelled, "you go back inside now, you hear? This is man's work. I want to talk to that Henry Sweet. You hear me Henry? You hear me Billy?"

"Mr. John Barrow . . ." Charley yelled.

"Now, Charley, you do like I tell you. Pig stealing and kidnapping's a serious business and Henry and Billy won't git away with it, I promise you that." He snuggled up closer to his shotgun.

"Henry Sweet, you had your day!" he yelled. "There's a hundred men out here, and you surrounded on all sides. We want the pig and we want Charley. Now I got a shotgun out here that don't miss and it's loaded with birdshot and you'll be digging shot out of your hide for a year if you don't do like I say. Now, what about it Henry?"

Charley stuck his head out of the door again. "Mr. John Barrow . . ." he said. But that wasn't the way Mr. John Barrow wanted it.

"Charley, now you better keep your head inside till all of this is settled. I might mistake you for Henry or Billy and this shotgun could go off and that would be a terrible thing. Now stay inside, son, till us men git this thing settled." Then he went back to yelling at Henry.

"Now, Henry Sweet, you got ten minutes to make up your mind to come out peaceable. After that all hundred of us out here plan to come in there and stomp all over you. Now, I don't want to hear a peep out of nobody until that ten minutes is up." Then he sat down on the ground and wiggled himself around to nest in. His shotgun was cradled in his lap, pointing in the direction of the house. When he was settled in, he turned to me and whispered, "Pinch, why don't you sneak around back and make some noise so they'll think there's more than jist two of us out here." He was enjoying himself, you could see that. It was like being a general on a battlefield, except that he had a one-man army, and there was more swamp than field.

"Mr. John Barrow, how you going to tell when the ten minutes are up? Neither of us got a clock." But he didn't get a chance to answer, 'cause the door started opening slowly again. This time it was Mrs. Henry Sweet's untidy head that poked out the door.

"Mr. John Barrow . . ." she called sweetly to him.

"Now, Mrs. Sweet, you be careful there . . ."

". . . we are coming out," she said softly, but there was no mistaking her intention.

He didn't do any arguing with her like he had with Charley. He just jumped up ready for action. His shotgun was raised. Henry and Billy could rush out blazing if they wanted to. He was ready.

"All right, then, if that's the way it's got to be, Henry and Billy you come out last and come out with your hands up over your heads."

So Charley came out and walked down the steps and over to where we were standing. But Henry and Billy didn't come out.

"Henry and Billy, why ain't you coming out of there

like I told you to," Mr. John Barrow yelled at them and let off a blast of his shotgun that shook the branches off the trees.

"Don't waste any more shells," Charley told him. "Mrs. Sweet says they went hunting a couple of hours ago. I was just in there having some tea with her. And Mr. John Barrow, she was telling my fortune with the tea leaves. The tea leaves said that I should wait for you 'cause you'd be coming by if you didn't get into too much trouble doing it."

Then the front door opened slowly again and Mr. John Barrow tensed. It was only Mrs. Sweet. She poked her head out smiling and waving.

"Got some more tea, if anybody's interested," she yelled. But nobody was.

"Mr. John Barrow, she said they were going to do their hunting around Blind River," Charley said. "What about me and Pinch using Mrs. Sweet's boat and cutting across the swamp? We could keep an eye on them while you went for help."

"I want Pinch to stay with me, Charley. I need him to git his paw to help us on this."

"My dad won't help, Mr. John Barrow. You heard him. And anyway, I don't want to talk to him anymore. I want to do some of the dangerous stuff, like what Charley says." Sure wouldn't be any fun in this if I had to stay with a bunch of grown-ups all the time. Specially if one of them was my own dad.

"Pinch, you stay with me, now. This is serious business and I need your help," said Mr. John Barrow.

"Well, you sure don't need both of us," Charley said. "I'll find them Sweets, and I'll stick to them like a leech. When you get close to the Blind River boat tie-up, whistle like a bobwhite. I'll whistle back." Then he turned around and went back to ask Mrs. Sweet for the loan of her boat.

❦ 15 ❦

Rescue Party

W E WERE heading for my house to talk to my dad about helping out when Mr. Tony yelled at us more like he does when he's deputy sheriffing than when he's storekeeping. Mr. John Barrow told him how the Sweets had almost kidnapped Charley and now they were hunting around Blind River.

"We could use some help in going after them. They'll be liquored up, for sure." But Mr. Tony didn't seem like he wanted to spend his afternoon doing it. He shifted to his storekeeping look.

"That pig ain't worth chasing very far after, John. Where is Charley?"

"He is scouting the Sweets right now," I told him.

"Well, I'd like to help you, Pinch. But I got some dusting to do. You find the Sweets you tell them to come by and see me. I'll talk to them about that pig. Right now, Pinch, you go on home. Your maw's looking for you."

But Mom was only trying to keep track of me, so soon as I had promised to be back by dinnertime I was ready to head off again. But then Dad asked where we were going and when we told him he wasn't too happy about it.

"I don't like the idea of Charley fiddling around in that swamp by himself, and his paw wouldn't either. Ben Riedlinger is working today, but when he finds out what's going on, he's going to be mad as a hornet. I changed my mind, Pinch. I'm coming with you." So the three of us put together some rope and water bottles and food and extra clothes and started out. And when Mr. Tony saw that the party was growing, he decided it was too nice a day just for dusting and he would come along too. I told them both that we wouldn't have any problems 'cause Mr. John Barrow was the best swamp hunter in these parts, but they didn't have the same opinion at all.

It turned out to be an easier adventure than we expected, at least the first part. When we got to the Blind River boat tie-up, Charley wasn't anywhere around, but somebody else was. The Sweet boys were there having a fine party, drinking whiskey like always, and singing songs about how their mother was good to them when they were little boys and now she has gone far away. That Billy Sweet had my pirate skull and when he wasn't singing songs about his mother he was holding up Jean Laffite and yelling, "Yo, ho, ho an' a bottle of rum."

That shoe polishy white pig of theirs that would never make it as a hunting pig was tied up to a tree and didn't seem too pleased with having to listen to their singing. The Sweets sang us a song about how the last time they had seen Charley he was over on the other side of Blind River, knee-deep in swamp, peeking out at them from behind a cypress tree.

Then Henry stopped singing and said, "I tried to give Charley a quarter to stop following us around but he wouldn't do it. So I stomped a hole in the bottom of his boat."

I didn't believe that business about him giving away a quarter. Both of them are too cheap to give quarters away. But they weren't above stomping a hole in somebody's boat. Charley would be in a real fix over in that swamp without a boat. Nothing but swamp creatures on the other side of the river to keep him company.

"That was your own boat you stomped a hole in, Henry Sweet. Charley borrowed it from Mrs. Sweet."

"Well, that was your hunting pig we left over there with Charley, Pinch Grimball, and the alligators probably got it by now." Then they started singing about their mom again.

The thing about swamp alligators is they can see in the dark. They wait for you to move and then they glide over and bite a chunk out of your leg. Or worse still, you find a piece of high ground and you sit perfectly still for hours. Then you look out into the dark and you are surrounded by pink eyes glowing in the dark, not doing a thing but just waiting. Charley might make it if he climbed a tree, but Homer didn't stand a chance in the world of lasting through a night in the swamp.

Mr. Tony said he'd take the Sweets back to town.

He would probably let them sober up in jail while he decided what to do. And he said he was planning on keeping the shoe polishy pig for ransom unless we could find Homer and give him back to the stranger.

But that must have started the hunting pig fever up in my dad again, 'cause he stopped Mr. Tony right there. He dug into his wallet and pulled out ten old one dollar bills.

"Tony, you put that silly pig in my pen. I'll do the ransoming while we look for Homer. If we don't find him, I'll fatten this one up a lot more and dump him in the cooking pot."

Homer had to be out there somewhere. He had to be. But there's even more than alligators out there to worry about. There's things out in that swamp that they don't tell you about even in storybooks. All I could do was some hoping and some praying.

I asked Mr. Tony to take Jean Laffite back with him and he said he wasn't partial to muskrat skulls. He'd do it though if I'd help him with the painting when I got back. I said maybe I would if I could do some of the real painting. Then me and Mr. John Barrow borrowed Billy Sweet's boat and set out for the north end of Blind River and my dad hopped into his own boat and headed for the south end.

"You take care of Pinch, now, you hear me," Dad yelled at Mr. John Barrow across the water, and Mr. John Barrow yelled back that he didn't have a thing to worry about.

But he did.

❦ 16 ❧

The Cypress Tree

W E CROSSED Blind River with him rowing and me
sitting on the front end as watchout. It was still water.
The only ripples from shore to shore were the ones we
were making. Mr. John Barrow knew what he was doing
with those oars and we moved pretty fast. I was having
fun trailing my hand in the water, feeling the cool.
Then he put a stop to it by telling me that catfish and
gars get real pleasure out of biting off boys' fingers.

Now, that's spoof, and you know it. He just didn't
want me slowing down the boat even a little bit.

"They believe fingers is wiggly worms, Pinch. And
they like to chew on worms and swallow them complete.
But I ain't even told you the worst part, son." And he
turned his head and smiled his crafty smile. I knew since
there wasn't anything worth bargaining about in the
boat he was probably planning to tell me some tall tale
or other.

"It's the Blind River Demon you got to look out for,
Pinch. You know what that is, don't you?" He was
being serious about it, and I began wondering if he was
spoofing or not.

"I don't know anything about a demon. That's scare talk."

"Maybe so, son. But I seen it one time. Now what do you think of that?"

"You want me to help you with the rowing?"

"No thank you, Pinch. I'm doing fine. I'll jist sit here and tell you about that old demon I saw once that lives in the bottom of Blind River."

"You want some drinking water?"

"Maybe in a little while. You ought to know about the demon, son. He's probably jist an old fish."

"Oh."

"About thirty foot long."

"Oh!"

"And he don't generally bother nobody . . ."

"I'm glad to hear it."

" 'Cept when they're in boats sometimes."

"Mr. John Barrow, you ought not to spoof at a time like this. We're on serious business. Homer and Charley are out in that swamp somewhere and we ought to be thinking about finding them. Besides, I don't like talk about a thirty foot fish."

"You're right about Homer and Charley, Pinch. But I was jist thinking you might want to know about troubles we might have even before we git to the other side of the river. I won't say nothing more about it." And he didn't. He just rowed. The only thing to hear was the water tinkling and the squeaking of the oarlocks. I kept waiting for something to happen, but it stayed quiet.

It was a hazy kind of morning, but I could still see for miles. I could see both shores. I could even see the north end of the river. But the south end turned around a corner and that stopped me from seeing it. Dad's boat was nowhere in sight.

All those shores were far away. Nothing between them and us but still, glazy water, like a sheet of glass. It looked solid enough that a person might be tempted to step right out of the boat and start walking. I've seen bugs do that. They do it pretty good. And I've seen birds than can run on water once they get up a pretty good start flapping their wings. It's a half flying kind of run.

The top of the water looked pretty solid, like the lid on a cooking pot. But underneath is something different. It's cool and clear on top, but down below it's cold and dark. The deeper the darker. There might even be a thirty foot demon down there and you'd never know it from up here.

The boat shuddered. I gripped the rails as tight as I could. The demon had to shake me loose of the boat to get me in the water, and I wasn't going to let him do it. Mr. John Barrow turned around quick to see what was happening. Then his eyes shifted off to the side of the boat. There was a dark shape in the water, bobbing slowly, like it was watching to see what we would do before it did something.

"It's only a derned log, Pinch. Too shallow here for the demon anyway."

I eased up my hold on the rails and started breathing.

The log moved off, still bobbing along. The sun busted through the clouds and things started looking less glazy and more real. A trout even jumped in the water ahead of us. I put my finger down in the water. It was cool. There probably weren't any catfish or gars down there right now. And who believes in demon fish, anyway? Mr. John Barrow's just passing time telling stories. At least I think maybe he is.

When the river turned into swamp and the water was too shallow for the boat, we put on our boots and hopped out. He tied up the boat to a tree and then tied a white handkerchief up higher to mark the tree. He had a pretty good plan. We would bring water and the snakebite kit and the shotgun and the rope. Everything else could stay in the boat. He said him and me would stay together, 'cause two is better than one in a swamp. We would follow the river bank for about a mile up-stream, and if we didn't spot Charley, we'd go into the swamp a ways and then come back down to where the boat was, keeping the river in sight whenever we could. No need for everybody getting lost in the swamp.

But it wasn't so easy finding Charley. For hours we combed that swamp every which way and we got tireder and tireder. The mosquitoes made lumps on every part of me that showed, and I saw more snakes than I ever needed to see. There was freezing water and mud and slimy leaves and soggy sticks in my boots. We weren't too happy about our searching. Worse still, we were at least a quarter mile into the swamp and

it was getting dark and way past time to get back to the boat.

"We better turn back to the boat," I told him. "You got a long row ahead of you in the dark."

"That's right, son. You lead the way."

"Mr. John Barrow, you are the leader. I don't even know which way is the river much less which way is the boat."

"Pinch, don't you worry now. I'll take care of it. I surely know which way the boat is. I been watching close. But the way I figure it, the boat's too far to git to, dark like it is. What we better do is climb a tree and spend the night where no swamp creature can git at us. Then in the morning we'll be fresh as spring chickens and we'll find that river fine."

I'd have bet a nickel he was as lost as I was, but I didn't want to find out if I was right. He was probably right about us being able to spot the river from up a tree in the morning. So we used his rope to climb up a big fat cypress and found limbs strong enough to take us. Then we tied ourselves onto the tree as best we could, so there wouldn't be any falling out of trees if we got any sleeping done. But I wasn't counting on any sleep.

This whole rescue wasn't turning out the way I'd figured it would. Can't go around telling your grandchildren about getting lost in a swamp and having to sleep in trees. The branch was already starting to cut off the blood to my legs and I had to change my sitting position every five minutes. Mr. John Barrow's long legs were giving him the same kind of trouble. I could hear him shifting around on his limb, but we didn't talk about it.

It was quiet for a long time. I thought maybe he was even asleep. Then he started talking.

"You know, Pinch, a cypress is a funny kind of tree. Good building wood. Stands up to water better than regular pine. But it's a spooky tree too. Likes sitting out here in the swamp all by itself. It's a dead man's tree too, Pinch. Why you probably didn't know it, but they tack cypress branches on a man's door sometimes when he's passed away. Shows someone inside's missing him." Then he went back to his thinking again. Homer and Charley were out there somewhere. Bad enough to be sitting in the dark twenty feet off the ground on a tree limb hard as an iron bar. Now I had to start wondering if I ought to break off a little cypress limb and bring it home with me in case Charley's dad needed it to tack on his door while Charley laid in a casket in the front room.

Then I started thinking about my mom and dad and what they must be doing 'cause I didn't come home. My dad would get back from the swamp at a sensible time and I wouldn't be back yet. So he would go talk to Mr. Tony and see what he had to say about it. Mr. Tony would probably tell him Mr. John Barrow was no stranger to the swamp so they ought to wait until tomorrow to start getting worried. My folks would talk some about it. Dad would fill a sack full of food and warm clothes and he'd set the alarm clock for before sunrise. Mom would finish supper dishes and take out her prayer book and sit awhile. Then she would go to bed and worry all night about her son who was lost in the swamp with that idiot John Barrow. She would worry about the deep water and the dark and the snakes and alligators. But she probably wouldn't worry about the thing that was giving me the most trouble. The more I settled on being just a little scared and sore from sitting on the limb, the colder I got. The later and darker it got, the closer I got to freezing. A sharp wind picked up. It kept the mosquitoes off us, no complaints about that, but I wasn't proper dressed for tree living in the swamp. I was one awful mass of goosebumps, and the best I could hope for was to get numb from it.

Cold gets you where you can't do anything about it. My ears were crisp as lettuce but if I covered them with my hands the cold crept under my arms and got me in the small of my back. My wet feet were turning into icebergs.

"I'm cold," I told him.

"What's that, Pinch?"

"I'm freezing cold. Might even be better down in that swamp water than up here with all this wind."

"Son, if that's the only problem you got, we can solve it. That's what friends are for, Pinch. Son, I'm going to tell you something my paw told me a long time ago. You listen." I could hear him shuffling around on his limb, trying to make himself comfortable. What was coming was that he was going to try and tell me his limb was like a feather bed and it was too warm up here for him so would I please lower the heat.

"My paw said a man's thinking ought to serve him and not hinder him. Now, what that means, Pinch, is that when things are bad, like right now, you spend your time thinking about how they're going to git better. There's something else I didn't tell you about cypress trees, Pinch. All day long they look up at the sun and they pull in heat. They do it all day long, Pinch. Then when night comes, there's so much heat inside that cypress it's all it can do not to burn to the ground. That's why they live best in the swamp. The water cools them off. You think I'm telling you a fib, son, you jist touch the trunk of this tree. Go ahead, Pinch, put both your hands on it. But do it lightly, son, 'cause you don't want to burn your fingers."

I was cold enough to try it. I touched one single finger to the trunk of the tree but I couldn't feel a thing. It was as though I didn't have any way of telling what my finger was feeling, hot or cold. Then I touched five fingers to the tree, and there was no doubt about it. It was as cold as a hound's nose.

"Mr. John Barrow, you are spoofing me again."

"Pinch, you touching the tree?"

"I am."

"Well, jist put your hand on it. Put your whole hand on it and keep it there. Put both your hands on it. That would be even better. Pinch, hold onto it like you was holding onto a big bowl of hot gravy. Hold it tight, son, 'cause you don't want to spill it. You got it? You feel how hot it is? Don't drop it now, Pinch."

I had both my hands flat on the tree trunk. He wasn't fibbing. I could feel it getting warm. The sun had been boiling the tree all day long, and it was no wonder it was warm. It was more than warm. It was hot. I snuggled over closer, 'cause I needed every bit of heat I could get to fight the chill in the wind. I could feel the sun's heat baking into me. It was pouring in. It was turning cotton into wool. I started wondering what I was going to do up here in this tree if I really started sweating from the heat. I never even had a handkerchief to wipe my brow. But I never had to find out, 'cause I leaned into the tree and felt the ropes bite in and hold tight and the branch I was sitting on softened up to move my mind toward sleep. The last thing I remember was thinking that it was nice up here in the treetops and that Homer and Charley probably weren't having it so good wherever they were down below in that dark, cold swamp.

⚜ 17 ⚜

Return of the Rescue Party

Early morning rain woke me up. It was gentle about it. My eyes just opened and I took in what was around me. Must be how a tree-perched bird feels. I was still in harness and my head was propped against a good spot on the cypress. It was the first time I ever woke up from a deep sleep twenty feet off the ground, and I don't recommend it.

There was still a light wind, and it pushed the rain a little bit. Didn't look like it was going to last long, but it had already done its work on me. I was getting clammy wet by the minute and the goosebumps were coming back. I put my hands on the cypress trunk to test it, but it was clammy cold again.

The river was easy to spot from up high, so that was one good thing. I sat still and watched it, letting my body wake up all the way. There would be time enough to find out if the rope was going to keep holding when I moved and to find out where all the aches and pains were going to be.

"You awake, Pinch? We better start moving back to the river and see if we can spot your paw."

But there wasn't any sign of my dad. He wasn't fool-ish enough to get lost like we did. So we sloshed back to the boat and rowed to the other side to see if maybe Homer and Charley had already been found. Mr. Tony was waiting for us at the boat dock.

"You did a good job, John, even if you did get lost in the swamp and didn't help much in finding Charley and Homer."

"Tony, my paw used to say that trying was worth something."

"Maybe he did, and maybe it is. But it was Pinch's paw that found Charley, and the boy ain't in none too good a shape after all that time in the swamp. Now you two go on home and get some rest."

"What about Homer?" I asked him.

"He didn't find your pig, Pinch."

It was quiet. Then I heard a single alligator bellow from clear on the other side of Blind River.

We walked down the road a ways. "Pinch, don't you feel bad about what he was saying," Mr. John Barrow told me. "We did the best we could. And Homer probably didn't feel no pain. But I'm real sorry about poor old Charley. He was wading in that swamp water with gators and water moccasins on all sides." Mr. John Barrow began shivering like the moccasins were after him right out in the middle of the dirt road.

"Gitting lost in the swamp ain't much fun. Look what happened to you and me. It's a spooky place in there when you don't know where the outside is.

You got to keep an eye cocked for swamp creatures and there ain't too much light to do it in. You hear noises and you jump a foot, and it's only a muskrat or maybe a crow. Sometimes you are doing more swimming than walking. Why, there's places ten feet deep, and deeper than that where the alligators dig theirselves a nest. But the scariest thing of all is not knowing where the outside is. You jist remember when we was up in that tree, son."

I left Mr. John Barrow when we got to Charley's house. I wanted to find out if he had seen Homer. But Mr. Ben Riedlinger said Charley was in bed and he'd be there another day or so and I'd have to wait until later to talk to him.

"But Pinch, he did tell me that after the Sweets stomped in his boat they yelled at him while they was rowing away about how Homer had been penned up in the woods behind Henry's house all the time. They never even took that pig to Blind River in the first place."

I didn't need to hear any more! I started running so fast a deer couldn't have caught me. I didn't stop until I was just short of Henry Sweet's place. Then I moved into the trees and cut around back to see what I could see.

The yard was bare. There wasn't a pig to be seen. It looked like the Sweets were off someplace, 'cause there wasn't a sound coming from the house. Then way in the back I spotted a wooden shack and I snuck

back to take a look. From off a ways it looked like a pile of boards held together by spit. But the closer I got the more it looked like a place that could hold a grizzly bear if the bear didn't want to get out too bad.

Then I heard pig noises.

Homer was in there, grunting and hopping around like a frisky puppy, and soon as I could see for sure it was him, I started doing the same. I knew it! I knew from the first I would find him if I worked hard at it, and I did.

"I sure missed you, Homer."

The shed door had a padlock on it. I kicked that shed from every side. It didn't look like much, but it was made out of oak and all I got for my trouble was a sore foot. There wasn't a way of getting Homer out of that ornery shed short of using a crowbar. I told him so. I told him that me and Charley would be back first thing in the morning. Then he was going to be a free pig and I was going to be a boy with two friends to play with again.

When I finally got home my dad said it was nice of me to bother to come home every day or two and he knew I wouldn't mind going to bed hungry this one time. Then maybe I'd remember not to get lost in the swamp again. And if I did, I could count on a belt-striped bottom being one of the prizes.

❦ 18 ❦

Mr. John Barrow's Plan

CHARLEY made it out of bed the next day. He was bandaged up like one big sore finger and limping on one leg. His face was thin and whiter than when he got that green apple stomachache a year or so ago. I told him about how me and Mr. John Barrow spent all that time in the swamp looking for him and fighting off night creatures from every direction. And I told him about how Mr. John Barrow said if someone dies you nail a cypress branch on his door to show that people miss him. Charley said it might be all right for us to nail one on Mr. John Barrow's door, but if anybody tried to nail a tree branch on *his* front door, his dad would hit them over the head with it, cypress or not.

He looked so bad I told him he could have Jean Laffite to keep for a while if he really wanted to and he said he wouldn't mind. So I loaned it to him. I never did like that pirate skull much anyhow.

First thing we did was to go tell Sheriff Tony what I had seen.

"You sure it was Homer, are you Pinch? Wasn't some other pig now, was it?"

I knew Homer when I saw him and he knew me.

"Well, son, it don't really make any difference. Your paw paid his ten dollars for that white pig and I got that ten waiting here in the store for the stranger to claim. Unless that stranger shows up I got no way to prove the Sweets stole Homer from him. Fact is, if he don't show up after some reasonable time, I might just have to turn that ten over to the Sweets, 'cause it's their pig your paw paid the ten dollars to get. That would be the legal way of doing things, Pinch. It might not seem the right way, but it would be the legal way."

Well, I had a couple of better ideas than that on how to get things straight. Even if I had to chop that pig pen down with an ax or break off the lock with a crowbar, I was going to get Homer out of there.

"What did you do to the Sweets, Mr. Tony?" I asked him.

"Didn't do anything to them, Pinch. Still got them locked up to teach them a lesson. I'll turn them loose tomorrow morning."

All of that didn't seem too legal to me. The Sweets weren't going to get my dad's ten dollars and then have Homer so that they could win the hunting pig contest to boot. Charley and me went to Mr. John Barrow's to talk this problem over with him, and it was a good thing we did, 'cause it was him that made me absolutely sure that one of my ideas was the best way.

"Now, you boys sit down here on the porch and

I'll tell you what we got to do," Mr. John Barrow
said. So we did. "Now, I been giving this some deep
thought and what we got to do is use some of the
Sweets' own tricks against them. You know what the
first thing we do is?" His eyes were wide and he was
rubbing his skinny hands together.

I didn't know and Charley didn't know but we were
willing to sit still and listen if he would only get on
with his telling.

"I'll tell it to you in two words, Pinch," and he looked
at me and then he looked at Charley and he waited while
the silence got bigger.

"The two words is boot polish."

"What two words are they?" Charley asked him.

"Them's the two words that are gonna do in the
Sweets — boot polish." He was warming to his story
now, really rubbing those hands together.

"Pinch, you remember how Henry and Billy used
boot polish to put that saddle spot on that white pig
and tried to fool your paw that it was really Homer?"

"Mr. John Barrow, you don't think those Sweet boys
are so dumb that we can use their own trick against
them?"

"Son, that's why this is the best way. Why would
they expect us to be using their tricks? They would
figure we would be using our own tricks. Besides,
Pinch, I talked to Tony about the hunting pig contest
jist yesterday and he said that the right time would
be about two weeks from now and everybody better

have their pig ready by then. So we got to do something right away to git Homer back."

"What are you planning to use for your pig, Mr. John Barrow?"

"Well, son, you remember the big black pig you and me caught in that pig hunt of ours?"

"I thought you sold that one with the others."

"Well, I did. Course I did. But I bought him back. That's a real hunting pig, Pinch. I can tell. I been training him almost every day. He's still got to be held onto with a rope, but I'm going to turn him loose any day now and let him show what he can do all by hisself. I might even win this year, Pinch. I might take that gold ring Mr. Tony's offering for a prize. I could hang it on a string in my house and brighten up the place. Course, Pinch, if I helped you enough gitting Homer back, you might want to go in partners with me on that pig and we could share the prize."

"No!"

"Well, son, I'm sorry you feel that way, but if you want I'll help you anyway. Let me tell you the rest of the plan. The first thing you do is to put a saddle spot on that white pig with the boot polish. Next thing you do is find out something about how them Sweet boys feed Homer."

"They aren't feeding him at all. They are still in jail."

"Well they'll start when they git out, Charley. Now, you and Pinch can go hide in the weeds and watch tomorrow. If they jist throw the slop between the slats of the pen, we got to do some more thinking. But if they open up that padlock to go inside, then we got 'em."

Now I've known Mr. John Barrow for a long time. He is pretty quick when he is dealing with you face to face. Nothing wrong with his thinking then. But when he is planning for next week or even tomorrow, he doesn't do so good. I didn't know what he was going to come up with, but I did know two things. It was going to be complicated and it wasn't going to work.

"Next thing you do is rope that white pig and hide near the pig pen. You hide on one side. And Charley hides on the other side. I'm too tall to be hiding in the weeds, boys, or I surely would be there hiding with you. When Henry opens up the padlock to git inside, then's your chance. About that time something's bound to happen to catch Henry's attention. Like a buzzard might fly over, or a hawk might screech, or something like that. Soon as that buzzard's got Henry's attention, Charley you stand up and start yelling — uh — yell "Fire!" That ought to make him look up. And maybe you ought to bring along a blanket or something to cover yourself up with so he won't know who is doing the yelling." He was looking at Charley and poking his finger at him to make sure Charley knew what he was supposed to do. Then he turned on me.

"And Pinch, when Henry jumps to look at Charley, you stand up and start running toward the pen calling for that pig of yours to git out of there. The minute he does, Pinch, take the rope off that white pig and both you boys and Homer run out of there. Henry will be twisting and turning every which way, not knowing which way to look. He won't even see that you are switching pigs on him until too late. Henry will be so mixed up, it will be like him helping to steal his own pig."

"Suppose both Billy and Henry go out to feed the pig?"

"What's that, Charley?"

"Mr. John Barrow, your plan wouldn't work in a million years . . ."

"Why, Pinch, it would too. I'm sorry you don't see how fine this here plan really is."

All that talk is what it took for me to know for sure that there was only one way to get Homer. Charley and me left Mr. John Barrow standing there with his mouth wide open still trying to convince us. I'd like to know how we were going to get that buzzard to fly over just when we wanted him to. There wasn't anything that complicated about my plan. And it started out just the way Mr. John Barrow's had. I put a rope around the white pig my dad had paid ten dollars for. I borrowed my dad's crowbar. Then Charley and me headed for the Sweets'. When we got there we pried a plank off the pen and gave them back what was theirs and took what was ours.

❧ 19 ❧

The Hunting Pig Contest

Homer and me went back to working the fields next morning. It was a happy time, just like before. We both kept learning.

The Sweets never did say a word about getting their shoe polishy pig back. I saw them working it in a field once or twice but it would never make a hunter. Last look I had it was a skinny pig with ribs poking out where you never see ribs on a pig. That was 'cause the Sweets weren't too keen on feeding it anything but table scraps and they were such greedy fellows themselves there weren't too many table scraps for the pig to eat. There wouldn't be too much competition there.

Mr. John Barrow's pig was another matter. It was lean but it wasn't skinny. It looked a lot like Homer except that it was solid black and had the same crafty look in its eye that Mr. John Barrow had. Pigs do that sometimes. My dad says that when a man and a pig associate themselves together for too long a time, either the man gets to look like the pig or the pig gets to look like the man. I hadn't seen Mr. John Barrow's pig in the field at all so I didn't know if he was a genuine hunter or if Mr. John Barrow was just making out like he was. But the pig had the look of a hunter and if I was going to get any competition it was going to come from that direction.

Soon enough Mr. Tony set the date for the contest and the night before I didn't eat any supper to talk of and I wasn't sleepy. I didn't even want to think about it but I couldn't get it off my mind. I don't guess anybody sleeps good the night before a hunting pig contest, even if you know that you are going to win for sure. I sat out on the front porch for a while watching the sky get darker and darker. Across the road there was a light in Mr. Tony's back room. He would be in there making the special copper ring which would be the prize for tomorrow's contest. I saw him make a ring one time. He sits at his work table with a hunk of copper in one hand and a little bitty ball peen hammer in the other hand. He puts the copper on a piece of iron he uses for hammering on and he hits the copper about as hard as he does those flies he flickers off his store shelves. He hits the metal again and again, each time so soft you would think he is scared of hurting it. Every few minutes he holds it up to the light to see how he is coming along. Then when he has pounded it and filed it and sawed it and burnished it with metal polish, that hunk of copper has turned into a ring that sits in his hand looking for all the world like it really is gold. It's a prize worth having, and all that stood between me and it was this one night.

Me and Homer decided to take a walk before it got too dark. We walked down toward the main road so that maybe Homer could sniff out a few field mice or sleepy birds and get in a little practice. We weren't out long when we ran smack into Mr. John Barrow and his crafty pig doing just the same thing. The two pigs rubbed noses and then went their separate ways, sniffing along side of the road.

"Can't sleep, can you Pinch? That's always a bad sign. I hope for your own sake you don't tire that poor pig out walking it around like that. The pig is going to need all the sleep he can git for tomorrow. Your paw never had to go against a pig like I got this year. You look at him over there sniffing at that tin can. He's a winner, Pinch. I hope you don't feel too bad when you lose."

Mr. John Barrow was always one for trying to talk his way into a winning. But I quit paying attention to that kind of talk a long while ago. And I wasn't interested in talking to him about anything else either. So I slowed down but I didn't stop walking.

"That's a boy, Pinch. Go on to bed now. Children should be to bed a lot earlier than grown-ups 'cause grown-ups don't need as much sleep as kids do to be good at things like pig training. Your school teacher surely must've told you that, Pinch. Take sickly old Homer on home with you and git some sleep and let us pig contest winners have all this nice fresh air to ourselves."

He was just trying to get me mad at him. And he was doing it.

"Good night, Mr. John Barrow. Your crafty-eyed pig's got as much chance of winning the prize ring as spit on a hot skillet. You save your craftiness for tomorrow morning at the IC Railroad property. Then we'll see who's got the best pig." I called to Homer and the two of us walked away from him.

"Pinch, you know about the school yard?"

"What about the school yard?" I stopped and turned back to him.

"Well, son. It ain't the IC Railroad property. It's nine in the morning at the school yard where the teacher makes her flower garden."

"I didn't hear that."

"Well, I guess somebody forgot to tell you. But you know now, and that's what counts."

If I'd have been sitting out on the IC Railroad property waiting for the hunting pig contest to start and everybody else was at the school yard, I'd have lost that contest sure. Not often I owe Mr. John Barrow anything, but this time I did.

"My dad would have told me when I got home," I told him. Wasn't any good saying thank you to him, 'cause next thing you know he would be trying to turn it to his advantage. It was time for me and Homer to get some sleep.

My bed has lumps in it, top and bottom. The only

thing lumpier is the dirt road out in front of the house. Winning that hunting pig contest was one of the most important things I would ever do in my whole life. My dad had done it until he didn't want to do it anymore. Now it was my turn. I wasn't as good at pig training as he was, but I was getting better. I was for sure a better pig trainer than the Sweet boys. They weren't pig trainers at all. All they were interested in was winning, not working at it. And I was pretty sure I was about as good at pig training as Mr. John Barrow was. He pretty often came out second to my dad. That meant he must be at least a little bit good at it. But the thing this year was that I had Homer and he was the best hunting pig there ever was. Dad says so, and I could see it for myself. There's a look about a real one. Anybody can tell.

I got up with the chickens the next morning. Even fixed my own eggs. And when Homer and me got to the school yard it was too early for anybody to be there. Except the teacher. No matter what time you get to school, the teacher is always there before you. That's the way teachers are.

She was planting flower bulbs. I don't know why it is that teachers want to work even when it's not a school day. She stopped working a minute when I got there and smiled up at me.

"Good morning, Pinch. How are you today?"

"Just fit as a fiddle," I told her. "Today's the hunting pig contest, and you know who is going to win?"

"Who?"

"Me. And you know why I'm going to win?"

"Why?"

" 'Cause I got the best hunting pig. There he is over there rooting in your flower bed."

"You better tell your pig to get out of my flower bed, Pinch. Otherwise he might hurt the bulbs."

I scooted Homer out of the bed and then came back to talk some more. "You know why he is the best hunting pig there is?"

"Why?"

"Because my dad trained him to be, that's why. And I trained him some too. And the two of us are just about the best pig trainers there is."

"There are."

"There are."

"Well, I sincerely hope that you win the contest, if that's what you want." She had gone back to working at digging around in the dirt, but she kept looking up at me and smiling every now and then. We didn't talk for a while. She tended to her work and I watched what Homer was doing to see that he kept away from the teacher's flower bed, if that was what she wanted. Although rooting in gardens was a natural enough thing for a pig to do.

"You think the people will start coming soon?" I asked her.

"Is somebody coming here, Pinch?"

"Why, of course. How are we going to have a hunting pig contest if nobody but me shows up?"

"I didn't know it was going to be here. I thought the contest was going to be on the IC Railroad property."

"They changed it right at the last minute. I almost didn't find out myself until too late."

She stood up from her digging and smiled at me. It looked like her work was about finished for the day.

"Well, I'm glad you did find out, Pinch. I'm going to have to leave now, but I wish you the best of luck in the contest. And you can tell me what happened on Monday when you come to school." She took off her work gloves and started moving away.

"Teacher, aren't you going to stay for the contest? Why, everybody will be here same as last year."

"You tell them hello for me, will you Pinch? I have some school work to catch up on." And she headed up the road toward her house.

I sat on the schoolhouse steps to finish off the waiting. A little more waiting is all there would be before a new hunting pig contest would be over and there would be a new champion. After a while I got up and walked around the schoolhouse three times. Homer walked it with me. But that didn't make the time pass any faster. I began thinking about what would happen when the contest started. They would take all of us out in a field, probably the field right across from the schoolhouse. One judge would go with each person and his pig. Each person and his pig would move in a different direction, pig first. It was how many times the pig could find a bird and point it that counted. They time us for one hour. The person with the most points in one hour will be the winner. Last year my dad got in ten points in an hour. That's the most anybody ever did. His pig just froze there like a real bird hound. Then the judge would throw a stone where the pig was pointing and if it flushed a bird, he counted it. If no bird flew, it didn't count. They didn't used to throw stones until they found out that some of the pigs were pointing at field mice, empty bottles, and just about anything else that was in the pasture that wasn't supposed to be.

About the time I was getting ready to take another walk around the schoolhouse, Charley walked up.

"Pinch, you know what I just saw?"

He knew I didn't.

"I was over by Blind River looking for tadpoles and who you think I saw?"

"Charley, if you want me to know, you better tell me."

"Why, Pinch, the Sweets were over there, and you know what they were doing?"

I just looked at him.

"They were waiting for the hunting pig contest to start. Now what do you think of that?"

"Now that's silly. The contest won't be at Blind River. Everybody knows where the contest will be."

"Well, they didn't. They said that they almost didn't even get to be in this year's contest 'cause nobody told them until the very last minute that it had been changed from the IC Railroad property to Blind River. But last night Mr. John Barrow stopped by and told them about the change. He said he sure didn't want to make it too easy for him to win the prize ring by them not showing up. They said if it hadn't been for him, they would have been left out. And they asked me had I seen anybody else heading that way."

"Well, he sure played a trick on them then. 'Cause the contest is going to be right here. And it's going to start any minute. Why you think I'm waiting here like this. I been here about twenty hours." I sure wouldn't want to be the Sweet boys, over there, with nothing to do but twiddle their thumbs while they waited for things to get started.

"How do you know it's going to be here, Pinch?"

" 'Cause Mr. John Barrow told me last night."

Charley started looking at me like I had my head on sideways.

"Pinch, you know where Mr. John Barrow is right now?"

"He's heading this way, I'll bet."

"Well, you would lose. He is over there by the IC Railroad property with a lot of other people and pigs. And Mr. Tony is over there acting as head judge. And your paw is over there mad as the dickens wanting to know where you and your silly pig have gone off to."

Now, I didn't believe that. Mr. John Barrow was a mean one, but nobody would be so mean that they would trick me out of winning the hunting pig contest the very first time I ever got a chance to get into the contest. Tricking the Sweets is one thing. That's just doing to them what they did to everybody else. But me and Mr. John Barrow were kind of friends and I didn't believe that he would do it.

Charley went off on his tadpole hunting, still looking at me like I was some kind of dumb mule or something. But I wasn't. And the way to prove it was to go to the IC Railroad property and see what was going on over there. I called Homer and started out but before I had made ten steps who should I see coming down the road but Mr. John Barrow and his crafty pig, and both of them were strutting like a pair of peacocks.

"Good morning, Pinch. It sure is a fine day, don't you think? I don't think I seen so fine a day since you and me did all that pig catching."

"Mr. John Barrow, when does the hunting pig contest start?" He was looking so happy I could see he was still planning on winning, but there wasn't a chance of that.

"Why, Pinch, I guess you didn't hear the news." He stuck his scrawny chest out about two feet and that crafty pig of his tried to do the same. "The contest is over, son, and you are looking direct at the new winner. We waited and waited for you son. Where were you?"

"What do you mean it's over? I'm still waiting for

it to start. I been right here. I been right here all morning just where you told me to be. You said nine o'clock at the schoolhouse and I've been here since seven. There wasn't any contest here, I can tell you that."

"It wasn't here, Pinch. It was on the IC Railroad property. Everybody knew that. You bound to have known that, Pinch." He was still looking peacocky, but it was kind of on-guard peacocky, 'cause he could see that I wasn't any too happy about his news. A person doesn't train a pig for a whole year and then get beat out of winning the prize ring at the very last minute 'cause another person tells him lies about where the contest is going to be held. I was starting to kick up dirt and he saw it and kept his distance.

"Mr. John Barrow, you and me were standing in the road last night and you told me that the contest had been changed to the schoolhouse. Now, you know you told me that."

"You wrong, son. You must've not understood me proper. I was trying to tell you the school teacher always digs her flowers at the school yard at nine o'clock when she don't have school. That's what I was trying to say. You jist didn't hear me right. But wasn't she here, Pinch? Didn't you see the school teacher here this morning like always? She sure makes pretty flowers, don't she?"

I stared at him. If I could've bored holes straight through his skinny chest with my eyes, I would've done it. I could feel the anger boil up in me until it made my arms tremble and my eyebrows curl. It was *my* contest he won. He wouldn't have done it without trickery.

I had my fill of his meanness. There was a bean pole lying in the dirt like it had been sitting there waiting just for right now. I scooped it up.

"What you planning to do with the bean pole, Pinch?"

I held it like a baseball bat. The skin on my hands burned, I was holding it so tight.

"I really wanted that prize ring, Pinch. You know, Tony didn't even give it to me yet. He says it's the first time they ever had a one-man contest and he wants to sleep on it."

He had his head kind of cocked to one side, looking at me. He wasn't sure if I was going to hit him or not. And neither was I. The trouble is anger starts out by puffing you up like a balloon. Then it starts seeping out. It was already starting to drain right out of me, down my arms, through the bean pole, and into the ground. But something worse was taking its place.

I was feeling hollow.

When you lose something you really want to win, it scoops out your insides. Then something good's got to happen to make you whole again. I was tasting the losing and I wanted to spit it out.

I wished Mr. John Barrow would move away from Four Corners and never come back. I wished he would cart all his trickery and meanness with him. That would take away the hollow feeling. Hitting him with the bean pole wouldn't help at all. I untightened my fingers and dropped the bean pole. Then I turned my back on him and walked away.

"Pinch, I got a favor to ask you."

He was following Homer and me down the road.

"Pinch, you think you could talk to Tony and tell him to give me my prize ring?"

I turned and glared at him. When I stopped Homer stopped too and Mr. John Barrow bumped square into him.

"Git out the way, pig," he said and gave Homer a kick in the rump. It was a mistake he was going to regret. All of the anger that had drained out of me into the ground came shooting back up again straight into Homer. He let out a terrible "Rooonk!" and charged Mr. John Barrow, knocking him flat! He bared every tooth in his pig mouth and champed down hard on that mean man's midsection. The only thing that saved Mr. John Barrow was that bad luck pouch he had hanging around his waist with all the silver dollars in it. Homer sunk his teeth into it and he must've liked the soft feel of it 'cause he gave it a twist and a jerk and snapped it free. Then Homer lit out like a blaze, streaking across the pasture and down the road.

Mr. John Barrow never did realize how close he had come to having his midsection chewed up by a pig. Instead of being thankful he just got madder still.

"Pinch," he screeched and pointed his bony finger at me, "you know where wicked folks go when they die? They go into the bodies of pigs, that's where. Boy, you got to help me git that pouch back. If you don't I'm going home and git my shotgun, and if I so much as see that ornery pig, this time I really *will* shoot him dead. I don't care if he *is* the finest hunting pig I ever seen."

When we got to my house old Homer was already in his pen. He was looking as innocent as possible, everything considered. But there wasn't any sign of the pouch. Mr. John Barrow slunk off red-faced and angry as a weasel, muttering so low I couldn't hear him even if I wanted to. Which I didn't.

⚜ 20 ⚜

The Locket

I TELL YOU, I was feeling so bad about losing the contest, getting kicked by a mule wouldn't have made me feel any worse. I had wanted to do it right. I wanted to win the contest the way my dad did it every year. I wanted to get the ring and keep it in my drawer. I wanted to be good at things the way Dad was and know how to use my hands and my head to fix traps and train pigs. I wasn't looking forward to telling him that his one and only son had gotten tricked by Mr. John Barrow again.

But since I was going to have to face up to it sooner or later, I decided to head for the IC Railroad property and get it over with. I took a shortcut across a field where the road turns. And that's when my luck changed. Didn't see it until I almost stepped on it. There lying on the ground was Mr. John Barrow's leather pouch, right where Homer must've dropped it taking the same shortcut. It was a pretty raggedy pouch as pouches go. It had been chewed on by pigs and I don't know what else. But it was still shut tight, and there was something hard inside. I pulled the drawstring open and stuck my hand inside, ready for anything from a blood red ruby to a black widow spider.

What I pulled out was a locket that wasn't worth more than ten cents. It surely didn't seem to be a good enough reason to go to a lot of trouble over. But maybe Mr. John Barrow had his reasons. It was an opening-up kind of locket, so I squeezed hard on a little piece of metal sticking out and the lid popped open. All of a sudden that silly gadget started playing a tune like it had tiny bells going off inside! I'd never heard this particular tune before, but it was a pretty one. When it finally stopped I wound it up like a watch and it played the tune again. No wonder Mr. John Barrow was so fond of his locket. He could have music whenever he wanted it. I tell you, if I was the kind of person who kept things that weren't mine, I surely would treasure this music-making gadget.

The only thing I really didn't like about it was the picture of Mr. John Barrow's paw and maw pasted inside. It was a tiny little picture, but plenty sharp enough. The meanness came through all right. Mr. John Barrow's paw looked out with black eyes staring at me like a loaded double barrel shotgun. He was saying, "You better git on over and give my son back his music gadget. Else I'm going to give you a licking!" Right next to him was his wife and she looked like she was saying the same thing, and not any softer.

There was a hole in the pouch where Homer's teeth must have torn through, so I put the locket in one pocket and the pouch in another. Then I turned around and headed for Mr. John Barrow's house. There was some more bargaining to be done and this time I had an edge on him.

When I got there him and his pig were sitting on the front porch. They made a likely pair. Mr. John Barrow was sitting on his rocker, trying to chew some meat off a rib. The pig had his two hind feet on the porch, his two front feet in Mr. John Barrow's lap, and he was trying to get the rib away from Mr. John Barrow. I never had to share a meal with a pig before and I don't know if I would care to.

When he saw me he gave me a cautious wave and the pig took advantage of his having only one hand on the rib and grabbed it and ran. But Mr. John Barrow must have known that the rib was about chewed out, 'cause he didn't put up a fight.

"You come to see me about my pouch, Pinch?"

I just stared at him.

"Well, I'm real glad you stopped by for a visit anyway, 'cause I wanted to tell you how sorry I was that you didn't git your chance at the prize ring this year. And I forgive you for being so angry with me, Pinch. I know boys can git pretty angry when they don't git what they have their hearts set on." He was wiping his greasy hands on his overalls but even when he finished I'd rather have shaken hands with the pig than him.

I didn't waste any time talking to him. When I got

about twenty-five feet from him, I took his leather pouch out of my pocket and held it up in the air and let it dangle there. It caught his eye pretty sudden.

"What you got there, Pinch?"

"What does it look like?"

"Looks like an old piece of dirty rag," he said.

"You want to buy it?"

"I'll give you ten cents for it." He started to move in my direction, so I jumped the fence and put a piece of barbed wire between us. He stopped where he was.

"It'll cost you ten dollars." I hopped back through the fence.

"I don't know why I bother to do it, but I'll give you two-fifty for it, Pinch, and that's about as fair as I can be."

"I'll take that for part of it. For the rest of it I want a piece of paper from you saying you tricked me in winning the hunting pig contest."

"Now, Pinch you going too far. I worked hard for the prize. And before I even git it you want to take it way from me by trickery. Son, that wouldn't be right. Pinch, your paw taught you better than this. I'll give you the money, but I can't give you no piece of paper confessing to something I didn't do. That wouldn't be fair. You know it wouldn't be fair, Pinch."

But I had him and he knew it and I just stood there, with the pouch dangling.

"Pinch, ain't we friends?"

I didn't say anything to that.

"All right, son, you win this one. But you watch out Pinch, 'cause a boy ought not be playing tricks on a grown man. I'll do what you tell me to, Pinch." He was as sad as I ever saw him, having to part with the money and confess his trickery at the same time. But he wanted his music-making locket pretty bad.

"Pinch, I don't have a piece of paper to write on. And I don't have a pencil neither."

"Mr. John Barrow, I came ready for your tricks this time. I got your confession already written on a piece of paper. Now, I'm putting the paper and pencil in this tin can and I'm going to throw it to you. Don't you come any closer. Then you just sign the paper and put it on the ground by your feet and put the two-fifty there too. And I'll put this thing I got down here on the ground. And when I say "Go!" you run to here and I'll run to where you are and we'll both have what we want."

So he did it, and I did it, and then I said "Go!" and he started running in his spidery fashion. I waited for him to get a good way from the money and the note, 'cause I didn't want him to pick them up and end up with them and the pouch too. Then I started running and when I got to where he had been the piece of paper was on the ground but only a nickel of money. And Mr. John Barrow was standing back where I had been, holding onto an empty pouch with a hole in it.

"Pinch, wasn't there anything in this here pouch?"

"There was a hole in it, just like there is now."

"Well, son, you got to give me back my nickel. You didn't treat me exactly fair, Pinch, charging me all you did for this little piece of leather." But I had what I really wanted. I stuck the confession in my pocket and started to walk off.

"Pinch, that confession ain't worth a hill of beans."

"Mr. John Barrow, they will put you under the jail this time."

"Son, you jist look at that note. Who's going to believe it? You wrote it yourself. I didn't even write it."

"But you signed it!" I pulled it out of my pocket to take a close look.

"But I didn't do too good a job at it, Pinch."

What he had done was to make a big wiggly "X" at the bottom like as if he couldn't write. But he could, and everybody knew it.

This time his trickery wasn't going to work. I still had the locket and I was the real winner no matter what, so I left him right then and he didn't come after me 'cause he couldn't have caught me if he tried.

✥ 21 ✥

The Copper Ring

WHEN I GOT HOME my dad was there, and this time it was me that strutted into the kitchen like a peacock. I had the best pig and I had a confession to boot. That "X" wouldn't fool anybody. Didn't make any difference that it was Mr. John Barrow who won the contest. Everybody knew what would have happened if a real hunting pig like Homer went up against a pretend hunting pig like that crafty-eyed one of Mr. John Barrow's. But my dad didn't see it the same.

"I never heard of such foolishness," he said. "I spend a whole year training a pig for a contest on the IC Railroad property and on the day of the contest you and him go rooting flower bulbs in the school yard."

He wasn't listening to any excuse about how Mr. John Barrow fooled me.

"Pinch, when a thing is important to you, you check it out yourself. You don't depend on somebody else doing it for you. And if you got half the sense any son of mine should have, you *never* let John Barrow be the one to do the checking. We talked about this a lot of times before, Pinch. John is a good man to

depend on in almost anything men do. He's a good
hunter and trapper. He's even a good cook. But you
put him in a spot where there is gain for him and he
starts making up his own rules. And all of them make
him the winner and you the loser."

"Well," I told him, "I'm going to try harder next
year. You'll see. I won't let him or anybody trick
Homer and me next year and we'll be the winners."

"I'm sorry, Son, but there won't be any next year.
We're getting out of the hunting pig business again
and this time for good. Homer will fatten up and bring
good money at the Farmer's Market. We're hurting
for cash right now, 'cause that fire in your room cost
us money. I wanted to see that copper ring come to
this house one more year in the worst way. It would
have tickled me pink to see you be the one to win it.
But if John Barrow's got it, then it don't mean that
much to me anymore. I'll stick to my work, you stick
to chores and school, and we'll both be the happier.
I'm taking Homer back again, Pinch. You are still too
young for this sort of thing. Maybe we'll try it again
some time when you're older."

I wasn't about to let that happen. It was me that had
the hunting pig fever now and I wanted to keep it. I
hadn't showed him the confession yet, but that's when
I did it.

"Look what I got here!" And I told him all about
how me and Mr. John Barrow had done some trading
and how I out-crafted him and got him to confess.

He didn't say a word for a few minutes. He just sat there looking at the note and looking at me.

"Son, this piece of paper ain't worth a thing. John was right. He didn't write it and he didn't sign it." Then he looked straight at me.

"You know, Pinch, that copper ring Tony made this year is something special. It might be the last of its kind. Tony ran out of copper when he made it. He says next year he might have to buy some iron ones ready-made. So this is a special one." He was quiet for a while. "But that don't matter." Then he stood up and crumpled the note in his big fist.

"Pinch, sometimes I think that John Barrow is having more of an influence on you than I am. Blackmailing people ain't right, not even if they did it to you. I really would like to have the copper ring. And maybe even more, I'd really like *you* to be the one that won it. But this time maybe we'd better pass it up. He used trickery to win the ring, but he won it just the same. Ain't likely that Tony will decide to have two contests in the same year." He walked over and put his hand on my shoulder.

"Pinch, I want you to do something. Tomorrow you get up early and give Homer some bird hunting practice, 'cause I changed my mind again about that. You train him hard this year, and next year you give the contest another try. You can be the first to win an iron ring and start your own collection. And listen to me, Pinch. Don't you fall for any more simple-minded tricks next year, you hear me?"

I was mighty happy about Dad deciding to stay in the hunting pig business. But I still didn't sleep too good that night, 'cause something else was on my mind. I hadn't told Dad about me still having Mr. John Barrow's music locket. I took the locket out and listened to the music a couple of times, but every time I opened the lid, Mr. John Barrow's paw gave me a hard look.

In the morning Homer had a good time chasing birds, but while I was walking the fields I kept thinking about the locket. If trickery was bad when Mr. John Barrow did it, it wasn't any better when it was me that was doing it. Besides, if Mr. John Barrow liked a little music now and then, maybe he had a right to it.

✤ 22 ✤

The Reward

LATER IN THE MORNING Mr. Tony Carmouche stopped by to tell us he had decided that a contest wasn't exactly a contest unless there was at least two people in it. He found that out in a book. There would be another hunting pig contest tomorrow morning. That's what I was waiting to hear, and the only one smiling bigger than me was my dad. I told them that Homer and me were going out to do some more practicing right now. Mr. Tony said that was a good idea. When he told the Sweets, they said they planned to do a little celebrating over the good news, but they promised him they would stop celebrating before the contest started.

"And what did Mr. John Barrow have to say about it?" I asked.

"Well, Pinch, I hadn't the time to go and see John yet, and I got a full day's work ahead of me. I was wondering if you would be a nice boy and go over and tell him. It's going to be at nine in the morning, tomorrow morning, in the IC Railroad pasture."

Before suppertime Homer and me took a walk toward Mr. John Barrow's house, but the closer we got the less I wanted to get there. I figured I had more thinking to do, so Homer and me jumped the ditch and went and sat down under the big oak. I told Homer about how I got the locket and how Mr. John Barrow's paw kept badgering me about it. And I told him how I was so mad at Mr. John Barrow that I was also of a mind not to tell him about the hunting pig contest at all. Homer sat still for a while, but pigs don't care to listen to people talk foolishness for too long a time, so he began walking around in circles just sniffing to find out what was going on. I kept on talking out loud and maybe he was still listening 'cause he would look at me every time I asked a question like he knew what the answer should be. After a while I knew the right answers too, so we headed for Mr. John Barrow's house.

When we got there, he was sitting on his front porch rocking, but when he saw us the rocking stopped and he just looked. That mean porcupine stuck his head out of his box and took a look too. Homer froze right where he was.

"Hello, Pinch," he said. "I see you got that fraidycat pig with you again. He sure don't like porcupines, does he?"

"Mr. John Barrow, I didn't come here to talk about Homer. I got something else to talk to you about." I told him I had found a locket on the road and showed it to him and asked if it was his. He put on a smile as big as a silly hound dog and took it from me. He said it surely was his and he was a mighty pleased man to have it back.

"And Pinch, I take back what I said about Homer being afraid of porcupines. I don't care too much about porcupines myself." He kind of whispered it so the porcupine wouldn't hear.

"Well, why do you keep it?"

"A man's got to have company, son." He stuffed the locket in his pocket where it would be safe. "Pinch, this is mighty nice of you, giving me back my locket and all. And Pinch, next year I promise truly I won't tell you no fibs about where the contest is going to be. I promise that, Pinch." He stopped his chattering for a minute. If I was ever going to tell him about the contest being tomorrow, this would be a good time to do it. "And, Pinch, the least I can do for you being so nice is to give you a big reward."

Well, I didn't come for any reward, but I wasn't going to turn one down.

"Now, let's see, Pinch, what would be a good reward for a young man like yourself?" He put his hand on his skinny chin and pulled at it like he wanted to squeeze a thought up into his head. "I know jist what," he said, and he went inside the house and came back in a minute with something in his hand.

"What's that?" I asked him. It looked like a big rock.

"Why, it's a rock," he said like he was surprised I didn't know it.

"I figured it, Mr. John Barrow, but what makes that big rock so special? Looks like a plain old rock to me."

"Why, Pinch, I jist don't have the schooling to tell you all about this here rock. It's a pleasant looking rock, though, don't you think?" He held it up like maybe it was a jewel and the sun would come sparkling through it. Mom says it's good manners to be polite to someone who's trying to be polite to you. She probably didn't mean for it to apply to Mr. John Barrow, but I took it anyway. He was making it easy for me not to say a word about tomorrow.

I started to leave, but right's right and wrong's wrong. So I told him about how Mr. Tony said the real contest would be tomorrow at nine in the morning at the IC Railroad pasture. He didn't look too happy about it.

"I ain't pleased, Pinch, but I been expecting it might happen. When a man's on top, everybody tries to pull him down. There ain't no pig better than mine. For sure not that fraidycat pig of yours. Now I got to prove which is the best pig all over again." He started to go toward his backyard. Then he turned back to me. "Thank you for telling me, Pinch. Now I got to go and feed my chickens."

Everything considered, Mr. John Barrow took the news pretty good. He didn't even ask me to give him his rock back. About halfway home I hummed that big rock at a blackbird sitting on a fence post, but I didn't have anything against that particular blackbird and I missed him good. If it had been Mr. John Barrow sitting in his rocking chair on top of that fence post, you can bet things would have been different. I can throw good when I want to. One time I hit a rabbit on the run with an oyster shell. You don't believe that, Charley will tell you it's so. He was there watching. The rabbit lay on the ground with a hickey on its head. Charley kept telling me how it was a lucky throw and I kept telling him next time we saw another rabbit and I had an oyster shell in my hand he would see how lucky it was.

Instead of doing all that talking, we should've been keeping an eye on the rabbit, 'cause while we weren't looking the rabbit snuck away. Rabbits are crafty like that. They are almost as crafty as Mr. John Barrow.

❧ 23 ❧

The Porcupine

NEXT MORNING me and Homer got up early. Mom fixed me pancakes for breakfast but she said I ought to go back to bed for a while longer 'cause the birds didn't even get up this early. But I knew that wasn't so.

"Pinch, you take care. Your paw and I'll be over later to watch. And I'll bring a basket lunch like last year so we can have a picnic when the contest is over."

I was hurrying to get out of the house so I could be the first one to get to the IC Railroad pasture. I thought maybe it would bother Mr. John Barrow, seeing Homer and me waiting for him when him and his crafty-eyed pig got there. But, he still got there first.

"Morning, Pinch. I see you and your fraidycat pig finally made it to a hunting pig contest. Not going to do you much good, though, Pinch. No use thinking it will."

I walked on toward him, but Homer was holding back and when I looked past Mr. John Barrow I saw why. He had brought his porcupine with him. The cage was sitting under the sycamore tree.

"Mr. John Barrow, why ever did you bring that mean porcupine?

"Well, Pinch, I *sure* didn't want to scare your fraidy pig. I guess I jist didn't think about that hard enough, son. The reason why I brought him is 'cause I wanted someone rooting for my side. Your paw will be here yelling for you, Pinch. And the Sweets will be yelling for each other. But there won't be one soul here wanting me to win. That's why I brought the porcupine, Pinch. I'll tell him not to bother poor old Homer."

The grass in the pasture was about a foot high. That's plenty tall enough to hide a pile of birds. I was studying it and Homer was sniffing here and there when everybody else arrived. The Sweet boys were loud as always. Charley and his dad and Mr. Tony Carmouche all came together. My dad and mom walked up hauling a picnic basket big enough to hold food for a Sunday prayer meeting. Even the school teacher showed up this time. She said she wanted to see for herself what grown men, boys, and pigs would be doing in a cow pasture on a nice morning like this.

When it was time to get started, I asked Dad to keep an eye on the porcupine, 'cause you never could tell what Mr. John Barrow would be up to in order to win the copper ring.

"What porcupine is that, Pinch?"

"Why, the one in that box over there!"

"Pinch, there ain't nothing in that box. I went over a little while ago and took a look for myself."

I went stomping over to where Mr. John Barrow was standing with his pig and both of them were looking proud of themselves.

"Mr. John Barrow, where is that porcupine of yours?"

"What porcupine is that, Pinch?"

"The mean one that ought to be in that box over there." I pointed at it so he would know where it was just in case his eyes were as bad as his memory.

"You mean he ain't in his box? I better run and see." And he hippety-hopped over to the box like he was expecting to find something in it.

"Why, Pinch, you right. I guess that porcupine *accidentally* got away. That's a terrible shame, Pinch, seeing as your pig is a fraidycat when it comes to porcupines." But he didn't look too sorry about it.

Then Mr. Tony yelled that it was time for us to get started and I lined up Homer, the Sweets lined up their shoe-polishy pig, and Mr. John Barrow lined up his crafty-eyed one. We followed Mr. Tony out into the field a ways where some birds might be. But this wasn't going to be a good day. We weren't more than ten steps from the start when Homer came across the porcupine's trail and he froze.

"You got to keep up with us, now, Pinch," Mr. Tony said.

I gave Homer a push and he crossed the scent, but he didn't want to do it. About five more steps and we hit it again. That porcupine must've been zigzagging in the same general direction as we were going. At this rate Homer's mind wasn't going to be on what it was supposed to be on.

"We'll start here," Mr. Tony said, motioning for us to stop. "I'll work with Pinch. Ben Riedlinger can work with John. And Will Grimball can work with the Sweets. I'll keep time, like always. Now, you three get on your marks and when I say 'Go!' you can start walking your pigs in any direction you want. Most birds pointed by a pig in one hour is the winner, like always."

Wasn't a way in the world to tell which way that porcupine was zigzagging. And for all I knew there was more than one of them in this field. If Mr. John Barrow had gone to all the trouble to get one out here, he might have gone to a little more trouble and turned a dozen loose. Homer and I didn't stand a chance against a dozen porcupines. Not unless something happened to change the odds. I kept talking to him to get up his courage.

"Homer, porcupines are nice enough critters when you don't bother them. You'd 'a never got swatted on the nose if you hadn't backed him into a corner. Pigs that have their minds on being scared of porcupines can't do a good job of sniffing out birds."

I wasn't sure he was paying attention to all I was saying, but I could see the part about him being afraid of porcupines didn't set right with him. He didn't want to be called a fraidycat. But he kept thinking about quills sticking in noses.

"Now, you listen to me, you pig. That porcupine's probably a mile away looking for a tree to climb. So you pay attention to what you're supposed to be doing."

I guess he had been thinking a little bit about it, all right. For sure he wasn't about to let on to those other pigs that he was thinking about porcupines instead of birds. He pushed his pinky-tender nose up in the air like it was made of cast iron and no sharp quill in the world could do it any harm. He gave the shoe-polishy pig and the crafty-eyed pig such a hard look they almost laid down and quit right then and there. But Mr. John Barrow gave his pig a kick and it straightened up and Billy Sweet did the same to his. Then Mr. Tony said, "Go!"

I knelt down quick and spit on my finger and checked the direction of the wind at the level of Homer's nose. My dad told me more than once it don't mean a thing to know where the wind is coming from standing up. It's the pig's nose that's going to do the smelling.

We didn't even have a chance to get started good before Mr. John Barrow let out a yell that made the ground shake. I looked over quick and there was that crafty-eyed pig frozen to a point. And standing right behind him was Mr. John Barrow, tall as a pine tree with his scrawny chest stuck out and his arms folded in front and a hound dog grin on his face. He was so satisfied with himself, it made you sick.

We all watched while Mr. Riedlinger walked over slowly and then threw a rock in front of where the pig was pointing. At first there was a rustling in the grass and nothing happened. But then a bird shot up in the air a mile a minute. It was the only time I ever saw a bird rising up in the air with a long piece of red string dangling from one leg. Nobody said a word about it, but I'll bet you a quarter that Mr. John Barrow had staked that bird out in the field and knew exactly where to go to find it.

"One for John," Mr. Tony yelled to the rest of us. But that wasn't good enough for Mr. John Barrow.

"You wasting your time out here in this field, Pinch. Won't do you a bit of good. No use thinking it will," he yelled at me. I started walking again but he stood right where he was and kept staring straight across at me and Homer to make sure we got the message. Then all of a sudden his eyes popped open wide and he clamped his mouth shut, so I switched from looking at him to looking at Homer, and that pig was standing still as a dead leaf, not a foot in front of me. He was froze in as pretty a point as I ever expect to see a pig make. His nose was out front, his bottom high, and a front leg curled up the way a real hound dog does when he's serious about pointing birds. Mr. Tony came up behind me and threw a rock and a quail as big as a turkey buzzard flew straight up.

"That's one for Pinch," Mr. Tony yelled at the others. "It's tie up."

But Mr. John Barrow wasn't having any of that. He watched that bird zigzag around toward the edge of the field. When he couldn't see it anymore, he stopped looking and started swinging his arms around and yelling.

"Tony, now you don't count that one. That was too big for a regular field bird. It must've been a chicken. Ain't fair to count chickens." But Mr. Tony wrote it down in his little book anyway.

Mr. John Barrow wasn't pleased at having the score tied. Him and his pig started angling over to our side of the field where he figured the birds without strings on their legs were and the Sweet boys decided they might as well do the same since they weren't getting any birds where they were. But Mr. Tony told them to get back where they were supposed to be, 'cause when things got started everybody had to stay in their own part of the field.

"Tony, you ain't being fair about this. Next thing you know, you'll be counting mules in Pinch's score."

"Be forewarned, John," Mr. Tony yelled back at him. "If Pinch's pig flushes a flying mule, I'm going to count it one for him." But he was only joking.

I leaned over and told Homer that he was doing a good job and to keep it up. Then all of us started out again. Homer was beginning to enjoy himself. He moved pretty fast into the wind with his mind one hundred percent on birds. Then he came across that porcupine track again and he flinched when the scent hit him. He picked up his head and looked in every direction. You could see that part of him was thinking about sore noses and another part of him was thinking about not being a fraidycat. Slowly his head came up high and he moved straight on. He was showing me, the other pigs, and everybody else he wasn't bothered a bit. Then he went back to sniffing for birds.

Wasn't more than a few minutes later when he froze to another point. Nobody said a word as Mr. Tony came up to throw his rock, but Mr. John Barrow must've sensed something was happening in our part of the field 'cause he stopped his walking and turned to see what was going on. The rock hit the ground and the bird flew and it was two for me and Homer.

"Two for Pinch, one for John," Mr. Tony yelled.

"Time-out!" Mr. John Barrow yelled from across the field, sounding like a sorrowful hound baying at the moon. Him and his pig came trotting over to where Mr. Tony was standing, knocking grass every which way.

"Now, Tony, something's going wrong here, and I surely feel you better do something about it."

"What's bothering you, John?"

"Tony, we all know that boy and that silly pig shouldn't even be in this here contest in the first place. I already won the copper ring one time. That proves I got the best pig. Now, is that right or wrong?"

"John, we took time out to hear what you got to say, so you better start saying it."

"Well, it stands to reason that something's mighty wrong here. If you count that chicken he flushed, that boy's got two birds and I got only one. Since we all know I got the best pig, something's got to be wrong. If something ain't wrong, how come he's winning instead of me?"

"O.K.," said Mr. Tony, "I heard more than enough. I'm stopping this time-out right here and now. Everybody back to his place in the field and get to work."

"You ain't answered me yet, Tony," Mr. John Barrow said.

"I don't plan to either. John. You better move, 'cause the time is running and your jawing won't make my timepiece run any slower."

Mr. John Barrow didn't want to do it but he finally went back across the field to his hunting place. I took a look to see what the Sweets were doing. They hadn't even stopped looking for birds during the time out. But nobody was bothering to say anything about it, 'cause the Sweets had about as much chance of flushing a bird as a flea has on a drowning dog.

Homer was really in the spirit of the thing by now and already his nose was to the ground and he was moving ahead by himself. He was moving so fast and smooth, it didn't take too many minutes for him to hit paydirt again while everybody was still watching. He froze into a point again and at that very same moment Mr. John Barrow made a spindly-legged turnabout and started heading our way yelling, "Time-out!"

But Mr. Tony had more than he could chew on.

"John, don't you come one step closer. This timepiece is still running." Then he threw the rock and up came

another bird. But Mr. John Barrow kept coming right
ahead.

"Can't I have a time-out if I want one?"

"You already had more time-outs than the law
allows." But that wasn't enough to slow him down
either.

"Well, can't Billy Sweet have a time-out if he's a
mind to?" He kept coming, twisting his skinny body
and beckoning for Billy, but Mr. Tony waved Billy
back. He was getting mad about all this. He stood up
there, hands on hips, chin stuck out, like a spunky banty
rooster ready to joust with a game cock.

"Listen, now, you boys think I got all morning to
stand out here in this field and run this contest? A man's
got to make a living. My store don't make a dime when
I'm standing out here in this grass."

I was on his side, but he was kind of stretching it,
'cause he didn't get more than a handful of customers
even on good days, and it was pretty certain that most
of his regular customers were out here watching me win
the hunting pig contest.

"John, you go back where you belong. The score is
three for Pinch and one for you. And none for the
Sweets, which is to be expected. We still got about a
quarter hour to go. You yell time-out one more time
and I'm going to call an end to all this foolishness and
go home and tend my store."

"Your ruling seems a mite fairer to Pinch than to all
us other fellows out here with pigs," Mr. John Barrow
told him, but that was all the grumbling he did. Then

him and his pig went trudging back to where they were
supposed to be.

Nothing happened for a little while after that. Homer
and me moved pretty deep in the field. We did it mighty
fast 'cause that pig didn't seem a bit worried about
porcupines or anything else. Then without warning he
froze and pointed again, and that's when we got ourselves a *real* surprise. When Mr. Tony threw the rock a
bird came streaking up, all right. What made it interest-
ing was that it had a long piece of red string tied onto
one leg.

I took a quick look over at Mr. John Barrow, and you
could see he was holding tight onto himself. He didn't
say a word, but you couldn't expect him to like it when
his very own personal bird showed up twice in the
scoring, once for him and once for us.

"Four for Pinch," Mr. Tony yelled, and we all went
back to our hunting.

It was quiet again, and it was a good kind of quiet,
'cause I was getting nearer to winning by the minute.
Nothing but grass crackling. Not a bird anyplace. And
then Mr. John Barrow's screech came tearing through
the quiet.

"TIME-OUT!"

"That did it," Mr. Tony yelled back at him. "Contest
is over. Pinch is the winner."

But Mr. John Barrow wasn't having any of that.

"Tony," he yelled, "you made that rule 'cause I was
calling time-out every time Pinch's fraidycat pig would
git hisself a bird. But this ain't the same at all. This time

there's something spooking *my* pig, and you can come here and see it for yourself."

"This is the one and only last time-out," Mr. Tony yelled to all of us, and he started over to see what kind of foolishness Mr. John Barrow was trying to pull now. So I did the same. The big black pig was just standing there with his nose to the ground, not moving a muscle. But his glazy eyes were twitching this way and that way. Mr. John Barrow was hopping in circles around his pig, yelling at him to move, but the pig wasn't doing it. Something was bothering the pig, that's for sure. Mr. John Barrow gave him a kick, but still the pig wouldn't budge. He grabbed hold of his ears and tried pulling the pig and shoving him, forward, backward, sideways, but it was like the pig was spooked. He wouldn't move a muscle. I've seen dogs freeze like that in piney woods when a copperhead was staring them in the eye. I kept looking at him and it took me about a minute to figure out what was spooking him. That pig was porcupine-spooked, is what it was.

"Move, you pig, you!" Mr. John Barrow gave him another kick in his backside, but the pig wasn't about to move. He had smelled porcupine right here. He wasn't a dumb pig. The porcupine had already been right here. That meant it's some place else now. If he moved a single inch, he would be some place else too. And that might be where the porcupine is. The safest thing to do was to stay put. So he did.

"John, we can't hold up this here contest just 'cause

your pig's got the frights. What's bothering him, any-way?"

"Tony, you want to know what I think?" Mr. John Barrow asked, yelling loud enough to make sure he was heard on the other side of the field. He twisted his skinny self around and poked a finger right at me.

"That boy over there has cast a spell on my pig. Otherwise why wouldn't he be out there winning this contest?"

Well, Mr. Tony had better sense than to believe that, but he turned around and kind of silly-yelled at me, "Pinch, you been casting a spell on John's pig?"

By then I had started thinking of myself as this year's winner of the hunting pig contest with not a worry in the world, so I jumped right in, feetfirst.

"Maybe yes and maybe no. But before I say one way or the other, you ask Mr. John Barrow how his pig feels about porcupines."

"My pig ain't no fraidycat pig, Pinch Grimball. He can take porcupines or he can leave 'em."

"Looks like he'd rather leave 'em than take 'em," I yelled back at him.

Then Mr. Tony decided to put an end to the foolish-ness.

"Now, John, you got to get this animal to move so we can get the contest going again. If you don't do some-thing quick, you're the loser. Pinch has already got you four to one, so unless you get pretty lucky or unless a real miracle happens and that silly excuse for a pig of the Sweets accidentally points five birds in the next five minutes, the Grimballs will be the winners again this year. I'm declaring the contest started again right now."

❦ 24 ❦

The Winners

INSTEAD of going back to finding birds, Homer and me stood right there to see what Mr. John Barrow would do, and the Sweets did the same, 'cause they were tired of chasing birds anyway.

Mr. John Barrow didn't spend much time thinking about it. He started hopping around looking for something to get his pig moving. Finally he borrowed a carrot off of Henry Sweet who had chewed it about halfway down. But taunting the pig with the chewed-on carrot didn't work at all. Then he found a sharp stick lying in the grass and that's what did it. The pig let out a snort and jumped straight up about a dozen feet. He came down on all fours and the shock of it knocked the glaze out of his eyes. He stood there for a minute and shook his head back and forth. When the fuzz cleared away he saw the carrot lying there on the ground and took a bite out of it. Then he went back to strolling around and sniffing in the grass the way pigs do.

Mr. John Barrow put a big smile on his face and looked over at me. "Your trickery didn't work this time, Pinch. You see there? My pig is raring to go, so step out the way and see how a champion pig gits birds."

"Time!" yelled Mr. Tony, looking up from his watch, and the contest was over.

Mr. John Barrow did a lot of pretty good jumping and yelling after that, but rules are rules and Mr. Tony told him so.

"John, it was your pig and it was your porcupine. You should've introduced them."

Mr. Tony turned to me and put his arm around my shoulder.

"You did pretty good, Pinch. Now, let's go over where your folks are and we'll figure out a fancy way to name you the new hunting pig champion of Four Corners!"

I was the winner!

It was me!

I was even feeling like a winner. I had done it and Homer had done it. We had done it together.

The minute Mr. Tony called time, my dad had started running about a hundred miles an hour and he was in front of us, breathing hard, before we had a chance to start out good. He was a mighty happy man. He was almost as happy a man as I was. He was smiling ear to ear and he stuck his big hand out in front of him for me to shake.

"You and Homer really showed him, Pinch. It'll take John at least another year before he starts thinking about winning from the Grimballs again. And, Son, you just wait. You and Homer gonna do even better next year."

Us two men walked side by side to where everybody else was. Charley was pretty happy about it. "You sure made up for the dumb mule trick you pulled by the schoolhouse, Pinch." The school teacher came over and said she was certainly impressed by my winning. Mr. Ben Riedlinger shook my hand and the Sweet boys did too. Even Mr. John Barrow walked over and kind of sheepish stuck out his skinny hand, but when he started talking about how it was *his* chickens I had traded to get Homer in the first place, I walked off on him.

Mr. Tony told everybody to be quiet and then he took that big, shiny copper ring out of his pocket.

"Son," he said, "you did a good job training the pig and you did a good job handling him in the field. You keep going like you are and you'll probably be as good a man as your paw some day soon. Keep working at it." And he handed me the prize ring.

It sparkled like a ring of gold!

There wasn't another one just like it in the whole world, 'cause Mr. Tony made each one special. I would treasure it like my dad did all of his. I walked over to show it to Dad and Mom. Mom took it from me and held it in the palm of her hand. She said she had been standing right here watching every minute of it and she was proud of how I had learned so quick from Dad about training and hunting pigs. She said she still didn't care much for pigs, but if a pig had to be around it may as well be Homer as any other pig. Then Mom went

over and picked up her picnic basket and carried it back to where we were standing. She stuck her hand inside and pulled out the biggest, most delicious looking apple pie I had ever seen.

"I brought this for your pig, just in case there was a reason to celebrate. He worked hard for you. Your paw told me all about that porcupine, so I know Homer put his fear aside out of love for you. Any pig that loves my boy has got to be a little bit different from the general run of pigs. So, you give him this pie." She held it out to me, but when I reached for it, she pulled it back.

"No," she said. "That's not the right way to do it. I got to do it right or I may as well not do it at all."

Mom walked over to where Homer was standing, taking it all in. You could see he was thinking being a famous pig had its advantages. Mom bent over and put the apple pie on the ground in front of him. Then she stepped back quick. She wanted to do it right, but she wasn't planning on getting any closer than she had to.

"There pig. The pie's all yours."

Homer knew a peace offering when he saw it. But he'd never eaten an apple pie before when he wasn't risking a swat with a broom handle to get it. He just stood there, head cocked, looking at the pie and looking at Mom. It was mighty tempting, but he wasn't sure it was the safe thing to do.

"All right," Mom said, "I know what that pig is thinking. He's got good reason for it. Let's all of us go to the other side of the big sycamore and have some of this lunch I brought. And Will Grimball, you can stop your fretting, 'cause I brought another apple pie for you to sample when we're done with the sandwiches."

When we got to the other side of the sycamore, Mr. John Barrow was first in line for lunch, but Mom told him to step aside and let the school teacher be first, so he did. Then Mom started handing out peanut butter and jelly sandwiches. I took a look over my shoulder to see what was happening to the pie. There wasn't too much of it left. Homer was a sticky mess and there was a slice of apple plastered halfway up the side of his snoot, but it wasn't bothering him at all. He had earned the pie, now he was enjoying it.

We all sat on the grass and ate sandwiches and I had a great time, chatting with everyone about how I won the hunting pig contest. I told them how you have to start out slow training a pig, teaching him a little at a time. I told them about how we started Homer off on a rope to get him to come back when we called him, and how we used Mr. Tony's hound to teach him to point, and how Charley used the willow switch to stop him from sitting when he should be working. Dad was leaning against the sycamore chewing on a sandwich and listening. When he caught my eye he gave me a big wink, kind of like he was saying, "You keep on jawing, 'cause you earned the right to do it long as you don't do it too long." He was probably thinking he did a good job teaching me about pigs, and he was right about that. I was catching up on him, slow but sure. It was a mighty fine day for me. It was probably the finest day in my whole life.

Later, when things quieted down I decided to take a walk home and put the copper ring in my clothes drawer for safe keeping. If I was lucky, I might even find a can to kick on the way. I finished off the last of my sandwich, stuck the prize ring in my pants pocket, and headed for the dirt road. Pretty soon old sticky-nosed Homer came trotting along behind.